THE ATTENDANT

by Ignatius J

Books may be purchased for educational, business, or sales for promotional use. For information, please email
anaquariusdreampublishingllc.website

First edition

ISBN 979-8-9917668-4-5

Published by
Editing by Chanekka Pullens
Cover/Interior Design by Lika

The Attendant

February 11, 2012

Thriller Erotica

This is the story of how young Antonio's, a promiscuous flight attendant, Mile High Club lifestyle landed him in a world of trouble. Born in the projects in Memphis, Tennessee, he was determined to get out and make a better life for himself.

TABLE OF CONTENTS

CHAPTER 1

Wake Up Call

SPLASH!!!

"What the FUCK! What the fuck was that? What's going on!? WHAT THE HELL IS GOING ON!?" I could barely scream.

My voice was hoarse and my throat dry from cotton mouth. I couldn't move. I was strapped down. The air reeked of thick mildew. Ice-cold water slammed into me, jerking me awake, and my entire body shivered as my teeth clattered together. I struggled to loosen myself from the ropes that were binding me, and to pry my eyelids open — feeling as if my eyes were glued shut from dried tears. *What the fuck...* I looked to my right then my left, shaking my head in disbelief. I tried to wake myself from what HAD to be a bad dream. I closed my eyes as firmly as I could, then opened them as wide as I could, trying to get a picture of where I was. Upon opening them, I saw bed mattresses lining up against every wall in the room. This excluded a small boarded up window that the mattress's didn't reach up to. I could tell that it was a window behind the boards because I could see light peeking through the sides of the board.

The room reminded me of a padded psychiatric hospital cell of some sort. The frigidness was all around me and it couldn't be shaken. All I could feel was the freezing air on my face and chest as my body shook uncontrollably. My underwear and pants were soiled and soaked, apparently from my own urine. I assumed this was because the splash of water to my face and soaking through my shirt was fresh, crisp, and cold. I was thirsty as hell so that water was much desired. The water missed my parched mouth entirely — just a few stray droplets clung to my cracked lips, barely teasing my tongue and throat before they vanished.

Nothing reached my stomach. The wetness I felt between my legs was cold and stale, as if it had been there for hours. The upper part of my jeans was stiff — I'd pissed on myself. I could smell that I reeked of urine. My finger was swollen; my ring dug into it like a fat sausage link tightly wrapped by rubber bands, and it was throbbing with pain. I looked down at my chest: my herringbone and Mariner gold chains were gone. I asked myself, *am I getting jacked? I must be getting robbed. No, no, no, that can't be happening. Why would they still have me here?* I didn't have cash, cards, not even my ID! Think. Think. DAMMIT! Why was I tied to a fucking chair? What type of shit have I gotten myself into now?! Why would robbers hold me hostage? THINK. THINK. THINK!

As I began to calm down, I started to regain a bit of clarity. I started to remember. I'm in a basement. I'm still in HIS basement! The room had the same layout as the room we were chilling in last night. Looking up, I recognized the pipes and remembered the exact same floor plan as the previous room. He still had me tied up to the fucking chair. Why though? Why would he still have me tied up? Why would he take my jewelry?

After having dinner and a few cocktails at Trap City Cafe', we went to the liquor store and bought a few bottles and some blunts. He bought everything. We drank and smoked for a while at Fourth Ward Park. I did most of the talking and got bored of his million questions, so I was ready to go. When we got to his house, we had some more drinks, listened to music, and hung out in the living room for a couple of hours. Our conversation wasn't about shit, just more of me talking and answering questions. The kissing was whack because he wouldn't fully open his mouth. He was just lame.

His house was enormous, which was cool, but it was tacky from what I saw. The living room had wallpaper on every wall that looked like it was from the 70's. The brass coffee table with matching end tables, and the U-shaped purple velvet sectional didn't make anything any better. I was very unimpressed. There's so much I could do to a big ass house like his. I would trash all the shit he had in there and start over from scratch. His profile on Grindr was weird so I should have known. Judging from his profile pictures verses seeing him in person, I thought I had been reversed catfished. He was tall, a chocolatey delight, and handsome, but he had no sense of fashion whatsoever. I thought to myself, *he could never be my man just by the way he dressed, and plus he didn't have an ounce of any swag.* Usually, older men had a particular old school swag that I liked, this nigga had none at all.

Topping off our drinks, I remember he told me that he was going to get himself together, taking his drink with him. To me, "Go get himself together" was the code phrase for, "I'm about to go douche." I've heard that one a million times, and I've said it even more. I asked him if I could have an ashtray before he left so I could light my blunt.

"No smoking upstairs. We can smoke and finish drinking when we go hang out in the basement," he answered, dimming the living room lights. Prior to leaving the room, he turned the television on porn. "Enjoy yourself, I'll be right back."

Thinking to myself, *say less.* I took my shoes off, sat back on the sofa, and reclined my feet up. His television had to be at least 100-inches. It was the only thing in there that was up to date. It was like I was watching porn in a movie theater; it was intense. I took a perk and followed it with my brandy. I sat there daydreaming about how nice everything was going, slow but nice. Twenty minutes into sipping on my brandy and watching porn, I pulled my dick out and started edging. The porn wasn't arousing at all, but I was bored and horny. White porn never did anything for me anyway, so I decided to edge to kill time.

Over an hour later, he returned to the living room. "Are you ready to take it to the next level?" he asked, leaning against the wall.

I couldn't help but think and laugh to myself. I didn't even know we had completed the first level.

"Suuuuure," I told him with a side eye, putting my dick back in my pants. Grabbing my glass, I followed him down a dimly lit hallway that led downstairs to the basement.

It was spacious with a large open floor plan, a living room with a kitchenette, four bedrooms on either side of the living room, and a bathroom. I knew he was into some ol' kinky shit. Upon entering one of the basement rooms, I knew right then and there he was a super freak. The room was a sex dungeon, like some Kandi Burruss and Todd Tucker type shit! Red LED lights outlining the ceiling, black painted walls, a red leather sofa, red leather love seat, a couple of chairs, wall to wall red carpet, and a red leather sex swing.

There was also a low standing pillory, a stripper pole in the center of the room, a full mini bar, and a mysterious black leather pirates chest sitting under the window. I was down for it all. I was feeling very sensual from edging, therefore, I was horny as fuck. Our vibe was getting better, so I was cool. At least that's what I thought.

He turned on some music, and I started dancing and twerking on the pole in an attempt to break the ice, hoping he would open up. Pulling one of the chairs closer to me as I danced, he sat down and watched me. He reached into his pocket and pulled out a wad of cash. He started tossing it up in the air, making it rain on me. Shaking my ass in front of him while I held on to the pole, he smacked my ass and grabbed my waist, pulling me to sit down on him. I sat on his lap and gave him a lap dance, rubbing my ass on him trying to stimulate his dick so I could feel it get hard.

"Have you ever got a blow job while tied up?" he asked, lifting me up off his lap.

"Nah, I ain't never had that happen," I replied, knowing I was lying. "That sounds hot."

He handed me my cup and poured some more brandy in it. I took a sip, sat on the sofa, and lit the blunt we had been smoking on at the park. I watched him as he walked over to the black trunk underneath the basement window. Reaching into his pocket, he pulled out a set of keys on a key ring. After unlocking and opening the trunk, he retrieved some ropes.

"Oooh, this some shit you must do all the time, huh?" I asked.

He looked at me with a smirk on his face, and said, "No, just for special ones like you."

"Oh, I'm special?" I asked him and took a hit of the blunt.

"Yeah, you're special, really special, Pretty Red."

At that point, I was intoxicated from the brandy, high off smoking chronic, and high off popping perks. I couldn't remember how much I had drunk or smoked, and I didn't care. I was more than ready for the freak show to begin.

"Come over here and sit on the chair," he commanded, standing behind the chair, tapping on the front of it with his fingers.

I got up from the sofa and walked over to the stripper pole, doing a few tricks before sitting down. Kneeling before me, he proceeded to tie me up. First, he tied my ankles to the front two chair legs. Interrupting him before going any further, I told him to give me another perk before he continued.

He looked up at me, while still on his knees tightening the rope. "DAMN! Fucking pill head." He frowned at me.

I remember looking at him confused because he hadn't talked to me like that beforehand. "Excuse me? Who the fuck are you talking to?" I asked, pointing my finger in his face.

"I'm just kidding, I'm kidding," he swore, with a dumb ass look of awkwardness on his face. "That's a nice ring. You're not married, are you?"

He reached inside his pocket, pulling out a small pill bottle. After dropping two perks in his hand, he told me to open wide. I closed my eyes, tilted my head back, opened my mouth, and he dropped two pills into my mouth. I followed the pills with a big gulp of the rest of the brandy that was in my cup. I tilted my head back again, leaning in the chair.

"Nah, I'm not married. I'm not the marrying type. My cup is empty bartender, if you don't mind," I said, giggling and laughing.

"I got you," he said, reaching for my cup and smiling. He took my cup and walked over to the mini bar.

"That's more like it, service with a smile. Are you hot? It's hot in here," I complained, pulling my shirt off. "Come over here and cool me off."

"Let me finish making me a drink if you don't mind," he responded.

"I don't mind at all as long as you do a good job," I told him as I licked my finger and rubbed on my nipples.

He walked back over to me. "I plan to do a great job. You just wait and' see."

"That's what's up, my guy."

Only my ankles were tied to the chair so far. He took a sip out of his cup and bowed down before me. Taking an ice cube out of his cup, he began to rub it around both of my nipples in circles, cooling me off. It felt fucking good and cool on my hot body as the ice melted and dribbled down my chest to my stomach. My soft brown nipples became erect and stiff. The alcohol and perks were making me hot, and he was making me hotter. He continued to rub the ice cubes on my hardened nipples.

Taking a sip from his cup, he then placed his cold generously full lips over my left nipple. My body trembled. Switching to suck on my right nipple, he opened his mouth allowing the alcohol in his mouth to flow down my chest, reaching my belly button and running into my pants. With ice still in his mouth, he licked up the alcohol from inside of my navel.

"Oh, we can't mess your pants up," he said, lifting his head. He looked directly into my eyes. After unbuckling my belt, he pulled my pants down to my tied ankles. Forcefully, he pressed his face between my legs and began sniffing and smelling my crotch. He moaned, "Mmmm mmmm." He then aggressively licked around the outskirts of my G-string.

Bearing down his nose against my princess made it stiffen and jump with anticipation of being sucked. He rubbed his face up and down and side to side against my musty sweaty underwear. It made my rock-hard dick feel imprisoned from feeling the heat of his face and the warmth and wetness drooling from his mouth. I started to whine with ecstasy. Grabbing his head and pressing it hard between my legs. . .

"Not yet," he told me.

Standing up, he took a sip out of his cup and handed it to me. I sipped on whatever he had in his cup. It wasn't brandy, I knew that for a fact. He lit another blunt, handing it to me after he took a couple of puffs. I took a few puffs, and he asked me if I wanted another perk.

I told him, "Sure." Popping it into my mouth, I chased it with that strong ass shit he had in his cup.

He picked up some more rope that was lying on the floor next to the chair that I was sitting in. With a faint kiss on my lips, he said, "Part two."

I said," Okay then." With a devious smile, opening my legs.

He tied my thighs to the chair arms with my legs wide open and tightly pulled the rope.

"Ouch! Not too tight!" I yelled.

"Well, now what fun would it be if it's not tight?" he asked, giving me a lascivious wink.

I smiled, and asked him, "What is the safe word, pineapples?"

"Whatever you want it to be," he laughed.

After tying my midsection and biceps to the back of the chair, he walked to the side of me, rubbing my chest. I looked up at him as he slowly walked behind me removing his shirt. He leaned down and whispered something in my ear. I couldn't quite make out what he said, but it sounded like, "You're going to remember this, Pretty Red."

Thinking to myself, *he couldn't have called me Pretty Red, only Jeri called me that.* I didn't think too much about it, although I could have sworn I heard him call me that earlier too. Well, at the end of the day, I was a pretty ass redbone. After removing his shirt, he wrapped it around my neck gently choking me with it. I remember wishing that he had choked me harder and a little longer. Leaving his shirt around my neck, he took my hair out of the ponytail holder and told me he wanted to see me with my hair down. With both of his large, strong hands, he massaged my scalp and worked down to my shoulders. When he stepped back in front of me, he paused — then flexed, his arm muscles tightening as he showed off his guns. I could see every cut of his chest through that tight red mesh tank — the dark hair, the curve and weight of him, and those pierced nipples teasing through like they knew exactly what they were doing to me. Indeed, he was finer than I thought he was from his Grindr profile.

Who posts pictures on Grindr fully clothed and wearing suits? The only thing that I found interesting about him was that his status stated he was 6'4", 220 pounds, and he was a total top. The fact that he kept hitting me up every time I had a layover in Atlanta struck my curiosity. The next time he walked in front of me his pants were off. There he stood before me, 6'4", oiled up, shining dark sexual chocolate. A stallion of a man with that tight fitting red tank top and a see-through jock strap with red and black trimming. The color red on his jet-black body reminded me of chocolate covered cherries when you bite into them. That made me want to lick all over him.

His face was sculptured and chiseled as if he was an ancient African deity. Thick and muscular thighs and calves like a football running back. I could see his dark ebony dick was huge as it hung low with protuberant veins through the see-through mesh of his underwear. It was girthy and long; at least 10-inches. The jock strap barely held all his man meat inside. His chocolate cakes stood up, round, and proud in that jock strap. Even his feet were large, black, and strong with thick veins flowing through them, maybe a size 14. My mouth watered, my dick was pulsing rapidly leaking precum, and my hole was hungry.

My mind was in a tossup frenzy between wanting him to untie me so that I could fuck him hard and long stroke his tight hole with his face smothered in that floor carpet. Or wanting him to FUCK the shit out of me every which way but loose in that sex swing. As far as I was concerned, we could have flipped and flopped all night. Even though his profile status said that he was a total top, my fat sexy juicy dick has turned some total tops into verse and even some into bottoms. All that drinking, smoking, and popping perks had me wanting his big ass with his big chocolate dick to DICK me down to pound town. He turned around and held on to the stripper pole as he separated his legs to the width of his broad shoulders and arched his ass right in my face.

His big, muscular, hairy bubble butt made my dick jump. Letting go of the pole, he used both of his gargantuan ebony hands and opened his ass cheeks, exposing his bushy tight little hole and tilted it closer to my face. I leaned forward in the chair to see if my unusually long tongue could reach his furry hole. He knew exactly what he was doing, it was perfect placement. Rimming him and stroking his musty anus in and out with my tongue was more of my pleasure than his. Granted, I knew he was enjoying it by the way he could hardly keep his balance. Turning back around, he faced me and kneeled. On his knees, he buried his face between my sweaty legs. Sniffing and smelling my sweet lady scent, he moaned and growled. Lightly biting my enter thighs he moaned and growled louder.

Finally, as he was unsnapping my G-string, I couldn't help but think to myself, *about damn time.* Removing my underwear with one hand, he grabbed my dick with the other. With both of his hands, he pressed my sweaty, precummed stained man panties against his face, smelling and devouring my essence. Slapping my princess across his face repeatedly, I could see the wetness of my precum on his cheeks.

Rubbing my meat across his face, he asked, "May I taste it? I've been waiting so long for this."

Stuttering with anticipation, "Ya, ya, YES, you may!" I finally blurted.

He started to slowly jack me off. Using both of his massive hands, he massaged my 8-inch shaft tightly up and down all the while using his drool as lubricant. Licking around the head of my dick, he licked up and down my stiff rod as well. Reaching down to my fat tight, throbbing, hairless, testicles with his salivating tongue, he licked and sucked on them. Slurping them one at a time into his mouth like they were jaw breakers drove me out of my mind with lust. It was intensively wild as my heart was beating out of my chest. Sweat poured down my face like a warm shower. My body ached with tension from expectancy. I wanted to bust a nutt in his face so badly. I wanted to see my jeez shoot everywhere. The more I moaned and squirmed, the wetter and hotter his mouth seemed to have gotten. I. . . I. . . I. . . then fuck, fuck, what the FUCK! The reality of the situation at hand came over me, as if it was a long-lost memory that I wanted to forget.

Raising my head up, I looked him into his bloodshot eyes, and I asked him, "What happened? How long have I been here? What are you doing to me? What have you done to me, motherfucker?"

He just stood in front of me with his arms folded, wearing hospital scrubs.

"Answer me, you piece of shit," I demanded of him. "What the fuck are you doing? I work tomorrow. I'm scheduled to fly out tomorrow!" *This fucker is on one*, I thought to myself. Why was he just standing there and ignoring me? "Man, what the fuck are you doing?! I got to—"

"Shut up, you frickin whore," he suddenly uttered before I could say another word or process another thought. "You have messed around and NOW you're about to find OUT! Antonio, you are going to find out what happens when you mess with the wrong nigga. Your whorish ass think you can sleep with whoever you want — married men included — and walk away untouched? Noooo, noooo, you little whore, not this one, not MINE! You got US messed up with those other fags you mess around with!

I know all about them and my fiancé is NOT ONE OF YOUR FAGS! You got all this WRONG, WRONG, WRONG!"

He was yelling directly in my face and spitting on me as his rage escalated. *What the fuck is he talking about?* This was my first time meeting up with this dude. This mothafucka is crazy. He can't be serious!

"My guy, we never fucked around. This is my first time meeting up with you."

"I didn't say WE messed around, I never said that. I didn't say THAT!" he replied, placing his left hand above my right knee and his right hand above my left knee before putting his face inches from mine.

I could smell the alcohol on his hot breath.

"But you did mess around with the wrong faggot, MY boyfriend, MY frickin fiancé! Now, didn't YOU?! You did do that, Antonio, didn't you?!" He gripped my legs tighter and tighter as the vexation in his voice rose. He continued to splatter me with his repulsive, hot, sticky saliva. With every word he spoke, the white foam in the corners of his mouth thickened.

"That lying bastard!" he said, shaking his head. "How could I be so dumb, so frickin blind! This is because of him! All this crap is because of him! I came out because of him because I loved him! I introduced him to my family! I loved him! I loved him and his family! My time, my whole world evolved around him and his family, not mine. HIS! I spent more time with his family than I spent with my own because I thought that they loved me too! I thought he loved me! I supported him when he wasn't NOTHING and didn't have NOTHING! I took him in!

He didn't have anything when I met him! He didn't have a car! He didn't have his own place! He didn't even have a high school diploma! He was working as a cashier at McDonalds for God's sake when I met him. The HELL! I loved him. I loved him so much. How could he? Why, just why?!"

Pausing from his rant, he picked up the bottle of vodka that was on the floor. After taking a long deep swallow right out of the bottle, the vodka leaked down the side of his mouth.

"I don't understand, I gave him everything. Anything he wanted, I made sure he had it. That selfish slut never needed for ANYTHING! I even allowed him to top me whenever he wanted to! I wasn't a frickin bottom! Do I look like a frickin bottom to you, Antonio? I wasn't even verse! Our relationship started with me being his top, HIS MAN! I picked HIM up! He was supposed to be the feminine one in our relationship! He turned the tables around, and I gave into it. I gave in because I loved him. I wanted him to be happy. I wanted him to be happy and satisfied with me. I didn't want him to have to find anything outside of what we had. After a while he didn't even want me to top him anymore, and I was willing to accept that. I just wanted him to be happy. Now he's YOUR bottom?! He didn't want me topping him anymore, but he frickin let you top him! Your punk ass! Make it make sense! Please make this make frickin sense!" Releasing his grip on my legs, he began pacing around the room.

"My frickin top, is your frickin bottom. Now what kind of nonsense is that? You're not even masculine. You are a fem boy, a queen. It doesn't make sense. This doesn't make any frickin sense to me! You're a stripper! You're a faggot! I screw faggot boys like you for sport! He rather for a faggot to screw him than a real man like ME! What the hell! I don't understand. I just don't get it. I, I just don't frickin get it."

He took a swig from his bottle. As he walked around the room, I could tell that he was drunk by the way he was staggering, trying to walk straight. He stumbled and knocked over the lamp and the light bulb busted.

We were in complete darkness until I saw some light when he opened the door to walk out. "HEEELP, HEEELP ME!" I screamed as loud as I could.

He slammed the door — a hard, final sound — and the quick jingle of keys told me he was charging toward me. His hands hit my throat before I could process it. Ice-cold, sweaty, crushing. The chair lurched backward. I hung there, suspended by nothing but his grip, lungs locked, heart clawing for space. "Shut the HELL UP! Shut up before I make your frickin eyes pop out of socket!" he yelled.

He squeezed my neck so tight, it felt as if my head was going to explode. I couldn't breathe, and I couldn't gasp for air to scream. I couldn't utter a single word. His grip tightened. *How the fuck did I end up in this shit? I just wanted to drink, smoke, get some good dick, and a couple of stacks of shopping money before my next trip. I can't deal with this right now. I can't be late again. I can't have any more violations. Delta is going to fire my ass. What the fuck man.* I just sat there tied up with all types of thoughts running through my head.

He mashed his face against mine with his mouth close to my ear. "Whore, I will unalive you! I want to end you so bad right now, but your ass is going to suffer! Antonio, you are going to suffer good and long until I find out everything I need to know about you and my fiancé! You are going to suffer for ALL this mess you caused me. ALL this pain. ALL this hurt, and ALL OF THIS FRICKIN EMBRASSMENT!"

Pushing me backwards, he released my neck. I fell to the hard, cold concrete floor. When my head hit the floor, it bounced up. Afterwards, I could feel the cool wetness of my blood leaking out the side of my head, running towards my left ear. I could hear my blood, and it freaked the hell out of me. I didn't hear him walking away, but I heard the door squeaking close and being locked from the other side. *What the hell have I've gotten myself into?* The dizziness took over; my head was spinning and pounding out of control. I couldn't focus, I couldn't think straight anymore. *Where am I? Who the fuck is he? What did I...*

I was out.

CHAPTER II

You Know Of Me

SLAP!!!!!!

"SHIT! What the—"

"Wake your ass up!" the monster demanded straight away after slapping the holy shit out of me.

I slowly lifted my head. *Fuck, what the fuck?!* Yesterday this mothafucka woke me up by throwing cold water on me. Now this fucker had slapped me so hard, I couldn't see shit but stars. My head was already pounding. He grabbed the chair by the seat with both hands and yanked me upright in one violent motion, slamming the legs back onto the floor.

"Why are you sweating, Antonio? It's cold in here. Why are you sweating and shaking, Antonio? Are you hungry? You want some water? I know you must be hungry and thirsty."

He knew damn well I was fucking starvin' like Marvin and thirsty ass fuck. Rolling his eyes at me, he walked out of the room. When he returned and opened the door, I could see that it was early by the brightness of the light from the sun that shined down the stairway. For a brief second, I could hear the gardeners outside mowing the lawn and talking. I used to hate that they did that shit so early in the morning because it interrupted my sleep. I fucking wished that I was in my bed sleeping now while they were mowing my lawn. I would get up and offer them a glass of water or some iced tea.

When the door slung opened, it bounced off that dingy ass mattress on the wall. He had a clear plastic cup that looked like water in his right hand and two slices of wheat bread on a white porcelain saucer in his left hand. I feened for it as my mouth watered. I felt like a crack head about to get a fix. Using his foot, he kicked the door closed as he walked in.

When he walked slowly towards me, I could tell his balance was off. *This monster was still drunk or was still fucking drinking.* Standing next to me, he tipped the cup of water between my dry, chapped, crusted lips as I leaned my head back welcoming every drop. I couldn't get enough. Water had never tasted so good in my life. I would have killed someone for some water right about then. Before I could even get to half of the water in what appeared to be at least a 16oz cup down my throat, he snatched it away. He balled up one of the slices of bread and stuffed the entire balled-up bread into my mouth.

"Enjoy it, chew slowly, because after the next slice, you are NOT getting anything else to eat today."

I couldn't even think about what he was talking about, and I didn't care. I just wanted the next slice of bread. Again, he tipped the cup of water between my lips. This time just for a sip to wash down that slice of bread, that sweet moist, soft bread.

"Open wide, Antonio."

I've been all over the fucking world, and I've eaten at five-star restaurants. Here I am now, sitting here desperately longing for some fucking bread. Before I could think about it any further, my mouth was wide open and welcoming it. He stuffed the second piece of balled up bread into my mouth.

"Drink the rest of this water," he instructed, as I was chewing and swallowing at the same time it seemed. "Hurry up and wash the shit down. Unlike you, I have a real job to go to, Antonio."

"Please, please stop this shit. I have to be at work too!" I begged him. "I can't be late. We did our shit. You did your shit. It's all good. I'm not mad at you. I'm pretty sure you got a good nutt off. It's cool. I got to go. You got your revenge." I didn't know what he had done to me, and at the time I didn't care. I just wanted him to let me go. "I won't tell a soul about any of this. I promise, man, just let me go. I got to go."

"Go where? Where do YOU have to go, whore boy? To have sex with the next sorry ass faggot?" he asked as his voice started to crack and rise. "To go screw somebody else's fiancé and destroy their relationship and destroy their home, like you've DONE TO MINE!? Where DO. . . YOU. . . got. . . to. . . go, An. . . ton. . . nio, huh?!"

"We can't go through this shit again, man!" I said with tears in my eyes. "I can't. Please, sir. I have to go to work. I must be in—"

"Houston, yeah, I know, you must be in Houston," he said, cutting me off. "Don't worry about Houston, Antonio, you're good. Unfortunately, Ms. Carla Nel, your mother, well, she had a terrible accident. She died, Antonio. She's dead and you, you need time off from work for bereavement for the next few weeks. Don't you worry though, I called Delta Airlines for you. Ms. Taroiya, your station manager, said to take all the time you need. So don't you—"

"WHAT?!" I asked in shock. "What DO YOU MEAN?! What the FUCK are you talking about?! How the FUCK do you know my mother's name?! My mama isn't dead! Man, stop this SHIT! STOP THIS SHIT! Let me go. Let me OUT OF HERE!" I struggled to squeeze my hands through the ropes, all in vain as the ropes started to cut through my skin. "I haven't done shit to you. I don't even know you. Pleeeeesssseee stop this SHIT!"

"SHUT UP! You know me, Antonio. You know OF me DAMMIT! You knew that he was engaged to ME! Don't try to act like you didn't know that! I have read ALL the receipts, Antonio! I have his text messages, dm's, and emails between ALL OF YOU! The Grindr account, the Adam 4 Adam account, the DIGUSTING VIDEOS OF ALL OF YOU on his OnlyFans! I HAVE SEEN ALL OF IT! You frickin knew he had a lover! YOUR ASS knew we were TOGETHER, and YOU KNEW that we were engaged to be married! And you tried to take him away from me. Humph, you tried! You frickin didn't even love him! You selfish little prick. You didn't even appreciate him! You were just using him!

The money that he was spending on you WAS MY MONEY! The allowance that I GAVE HIM! That Mercedes that he was letting YOU DRIVE is MY CAR! The title is in MY NAME! He was just another one of your flings! I know all about your flings and your little hook-ups. You got hoes in different area codes! You got them from all over, don't cha, Antonio? Even overseas, ya nasty little prick. Yeah, Pretty Red, you're a around the way hoe. See, I see through you. I know who you are. I know what you're about, and I also know you aren't anything but a wanna be. I have done my research! You're a broke ass hood rat from the ghetto trying to be something better than what you really are. You are from the projects that your hood rat mammy was born in by her hood rat mammy and birthed and raised you in.

A line of hood rats is where you come from, Antonio. Hoes, pimps, alcoholics, and drug addicts! Your whole family ain't nothing! Yet, you're still out here trying to live like you're something, and you are NOTHING! You think you're so frickin pretty because of your light skin, pretty hair, and pretty eyes! Strutting around like a peacock getting things on pretty privilege. I can't do anything about your eyes unless I pluck them out but that would be too messy! I could sew them shut or glue them shut with Gorilla Glue. Now that's a thought, mmmhh?"

"You sound like you're jealous or something!" I said.

"Jealous?! Jealous of what, Antonio?! Jealous of you? Oooooh, I'm going to show you how jealous I am, Antonio! Do you like my bald head? I think you would look good with one just like mine! Don't you think so? Well, what do you think, Antonio? Do you think you would still be a pretty boy with a bald head like mine?"

"No, man, I, I don't think so! Mister, whatever you're th… thinking about doing, please don't do it!"

"Well, I do think so. I think you would look really good with a bald head, Antonio. I'll be right back.

"No, no, please don't. You're right, I have been selfish. You… you… you're right about everything, sir. Please don't do anything crazy!"

He quickly walked out of the room, leaving the door open as I sat there tied up to the chair. I was afraid to scream for help again because of what he might do to me. My mind was running amuck nonstop. I started having a panic attack; I was sweating with chills and trembling. What was he going to do? As quickly as he left the room, he returned holding scissors in his right hand. With his left hand, he closed the door behind him. Swiftly approaching me before I could say anything, he began cutting my hair.

Screaming, yelling, crying, and struggling, I pleaded with him, "Please stop, please stop! Please, don't cut my hair!"

Tears ran down my face as I wrestled to free myself from the ropes. He paid me no mind or mercy as he tightly held my neck and snipped away my beautiful hair. As my hair fell onto my lap, so did my tears as I screamed and cursed at him to stop.

"You better calm down before you make me cut into your scalp, Antonio!"

"AAAWWWW!" I screamed as he cut into my skin.

"I told your ass to be still! That's your fault! Be still dammit, or I'll do it again!

I could feel my blood trickling down my head to the back of my neck.

"Ooooh, you are just going to love your new haircut. It's so becoming of who you truly are. You see, Antoino, I know more about your whorish ass than you know about your own trifling self. We're going to find that out right NOW!"

SLAP!!!!!!

"Aww, SHIT!" I yelled.

He slapped me on the same side of my face, busting my lip. I could taste the blood on my tongue. Fuuuuck, I felt myself pissing again. My head was ringing and pounding. This shit isn't right. This shit can't be happening. What the fuck did I ever do this guy? WHAT THE FUCK?! How did he know so much about me and my family? I've never told anyone about my family, not even Jerimiah! Whoever this mothafucka is, I'm gonna kill him the first chance I get. I swear it. I swear it on my mama. I'm going to slit his motherfucking throat. My head was spinning, and the room was spinning faster. Uncontrollable dizziness and nausea had set in. I could no longer focus, my head was heavy, and I could no longer hold it up. I was out. . .

CHAPTER III

The Bath

"WAKE UP DAMMIT!" the monster yelled.

Hearing that man's voice again gave me chills and made me cry. Him waking me up again made me want to die, but all I could do was sit there and sigh. I was just a pathetic lump of myself. DAMN, I was still damp, cold, thirsty, and hungry. I was confused and mad as hell, but there wasn't shit that I could do about any of it. My head was hurting terribly, my back, arms, and legs ached with unbearable pain. Never in my life had I been in so much pain. I had such a horrific stench, I could barely take it. There were many times when I had to shower with cold water and no soap, but I showered. I didn't go around dirty and funky. I can't still be here. Seriously this shit CANNOT be happening to me. The only bright side of it all, I was glad that it wasn't cold ass water waking me up or his heavy hard ass hand striking me across my fucking face again.

"It's time for a bath," he said, as if he was exhausted. "Your ass stink and you need to bathe. My entire basement reeks of your nastiness. Your smell lingers all the way upstairs. It's making me sick to my stomach, and I cannot take it anymore! I have to go to work today, so we're going to make this sweet and simple. Don't try anything stupid or you will definitely regret it, I'll make sure of it! See, Antonio, I have a real job that I must go to. I'm not just some whore waitress in the sky handing out peanuts for a living like you guys!"

I didn't care what the fuck he was talking about. I just wanted to get those sticky, funky clothes off me and the piss and funk washed off me. I also wanted something to eat, anything to eat. Feeling that hungry reminded me of my childhood and that made me more depressed. We would have at most a box of old baking soda in the refrigerator and condiments majority of the time. Cupboards with outdated seasonings and our pantry with crumbs of what was once there. The embarrassment of receiving electricity in the living room and kitchen through an extension cord connected to the downstairs neighbor's apartment became a norm for us.

Although I went through all of that bullshit, I still miss my family. Not knowing if my mama and my family were okay weighed steadily on my mind. Was this monster lying to me just to get a reaction out of me? Why would he tell me something like that? On top of everything that I was going through, only GOD and I knew how bad my body was feeling and how much I needed to shit. That confused me for a minute. I knew I didn't have anything to eat and drink except that bread and water yesterday.

Meanwhile, I was cramping and felt like I was going to lose my bowels. Why did my stomach feel so full and why did I have the bubble guts? How long have I really been down here in this man's basement? Why the fuck am I HERE?! I don't understand. I don't understand any of this. The more I strained myself trying to figure out what the fuck was going on, the more my eyes swelled up with tears. Fighting back from crying and letting this monster win, I had to think. *Think, dammit, remember.*

Grindr is where I met him, I certainly remember that. He was corny as fuck with a weird ass profile. In his first picture, he was wearing a powder-blue, baggy, outdated ass suit. He was leaning against an old ass blue Pontiac Grand Prix. It was the type of suit my daddy would have worn. The second picture? A large black long-sleeve shirt, blue cargo shorts hanging past his knees, white tube socks up to his knees, with old man Jesus sandals on. I almost got secondhand embarrassment just looking at it. He was hanging on the side of a swimming pool in the last picture. I couldn't see his body because it was partially under water, and I couldn't really see his face because he had swim goggles on. I call to mind the only reason I even gave Max a chance was... Max, his name is Max. MaxTOP 4ATL was his profile name, I remember. That's right, he kept hitting me up and I kept leaving him on read... until I didn't.

All the while he kept trying to convince me that his pockets were fat and deep. A bitch like me loves a nice bag and to shop. I asked him if he was generous, and he assured me that he was very generous. Wanting Max to put his money where his mouth was, I told him to run me some coins to my Cash App or Zelle. Him promptly doing so with a quick $500 to my Zelle account was a good start for me to get to see what was up with him. The same evening, which was a Friday, we made arrangements to link up the next time I flew into Hartsfield- Jackson Airport for a two-day layover.

I arrived in Atlanta that following Wednesday around 3:00 p.m. I was tired, but ready to get to the bag and have some fun. The Airport was only 12 miles from the Omni Hotel, but the fucking ride took damn near an hour and a half because of the traffic — which pissed me off. All the anger melted away once I got to the Omni. The Omni girls never disappointed me when it came to treating me like the grand diva that I am. Immediately after my glamorous entrance into my suite, I dropped my LV bags, my uniform, and everything underneath it right at the front door. I loved running around in my suite butt ass naked and free. With no work or bullshit for the next two days, I was ready to get it in.

So, while I was getting ready for my lil booty call with Max, I played some Toni Braxton on my Spotify play list. *He Wasn't Man Enough* always went hard and got me in the mood for demon time. Max claimed to be a total top, so I douched just in case I wanted some dick. *It's better to be ready than to have to get ready at the last minute.* Soon after relieving myself, I took a much-needed hot shower and bath. Showering first, then soaking in my Eucalyptus Bath Frizz while sipping on my brandy was always my ultimate luxurious way of relaxing. Laying in that warm frizzy water listening to Toni calmed my nerves and put me in a trance. I fixed me another drink after my bath. Chillaxin on the balcony

22 stories high with nothing but my robe and pink fuzzy slippers on had me feeling sexy and ready.

The view of Atlanta at dusk was stunningly breathtaking, and I loved it. Leaning over the railing with my robe flowing open from the warm Atlanta breeze exposing my nakedness to the world without a concern in my mind was one of my favorite things to do on the balcony at the Omni. I smoked a Black & Mild Wine wood tip and sipped on some more Courvoisier. It felt good, and I felt free. My cell beeped while I was sitting by the table rubbing mango oil on my sexy ass legs. I reached over and checked it. Cool, Max was on his way over to pick me up. Condoms check, lube check, perks check. Oooh, shit let me check my. . .

Interrupting my thoughts

"I don't want any stuff from you, Antonio, when I take this rope off. I got something for you if you try to trip out! I'll be right back," Max said with a stern expression on his face as he walked out of the room.

He reentered into the room slowly after what seemed to me like only a few minutes. But I dozed off, so I wasn't sure how long he was gone for. Max was pushing a black plastic cart with a silver metal tray with two handles on top of it. I couldn't quite see what was on the tray. I noticed he changed clothes and was wearing a white paper lab coat that doctors wear over their clothes, scrubs, and white tennis shoes. He also had on a pair of purple latex gloves. *Is he a fucking doctor?* I wondered.

As he walked closer to me, my heart started to beat faster. My anxiety was up, I could feel my body shaking uncontrollably. He parked the cart next to me. I saw what was on the silver tray: napkins, a box of those latex gloves, two syringes, what looked like a pair of medical scissors, a scalpel, a bottle of rubbing alcohol, a bag of cotton balls, and a fly squatter? What the hell was he doing with all this shit? It was weird, especially the fly squatter. I hadn't seen any flies or mosquitos flying around. All of it was just fucking weird and terrifying.

"Why are you shaking? Are you scared?" Max sarcastically asked, both of his hands resting inside of his coat pockets.

"Are you a doctor or som... so... something?" I stuttered.

"Na, na, no, I'm not, I... I... I'm a nurse," he laughed as he mocked.

"Man, wa... wa... what are you bou... bout ta... ta... to do to me?" I asked as trepidation set in, and I began to shudder as if I was having convulsions.

"Well, Antonio Diego Hillcrest, or should I call you by your stripper's name Ms. Ataraxia? Or should I just call you Ms. Antonio like all your good judies do down in Memphis?" Max asked, seemly trying to be funny.

How does this nigga know all my business?

"As I said before, your funky ass needs a bath. SOOO, I have two hypodermic needles here to help you and me out. The one with the orange top..." He pointed to the needle with the orange top on the silver tray. "It is going to help you relax and take the pain away. I know your legs must be cramping up from sitting in that chair. It's going to make you feel reeeeaal good! It works as a truth serum also just to let you know. It sets your mind at ease. So, before we have our little talk tomorrow, I'll be giving you this one again AND I expect nothing but honesty from you, Antonio! Today, I'm going to use it just to help you relax and relieve some of your pain.

Now, this needle right here..." He grabbed the needle with the red top and placed it in my face. "This one will knock YOU completely out. There's no doubt about it." He pointed the needle closer towards me. "You will be here even longer if you act up and make me give you this again! It usually puts a person in a comatose state for days, even up to a week! I've learned the right dosage keeps you under for about five days. So, your ass—"

"FIVE DAYS! What do you mean it keeps ME under for five days?! I've only been here THREE DAYS! Today is Friday, right?! Is it Friday or Saturday?" I knew my memory was a little foggy, but DAMN! "You picked me up from the Omni Wednesday night. We stopped by the Peachtree liquor store. You bought me some brandy and bought you a bottle of Clits or some shit—"

"It was Clix Vodka, dumb ass!" Max said, cutting me off as if he was annoyed. "Something your broke ass would never be able to afford! Yeah, I bought EVERYTHING because you said you left your wallet at the hotel."

I knew he wasn't lying because I always use that same excuse to get corny niggas like him to pay for the shit I wanted. Me paying for things that I needed was very rare but me paying for things that I wanted was not happening. If niggas wanted my time or more specifically some ass or dick from me, coins were most definitely expected.

"While I had you sedated, I went back to your hotel room, retrieved all your belongings and checked you out. To answer your question, Antonio, NO, today is not Friday, and it is not Saturday. It's Wednesday! Yes, your funky, disgusting ass has been here in my home for a week!"

My heart dropped as well as my mouth. My eyes began to swell with tears. This mothafucka really is crazy.

"We do not have time for this back down memory lane crap!" Max said, getting bothered. "So, are you going to cooperate and take the orange needle, or do I have to administer the red one again? The choice is yours, Antonio."

"Max, how long are you planning on keep me here?!" I demanded, struggling against the ropes like an idiot. "What's your purpose? What is the purpose of all of this?"

"RED ONE IT IS THEN!" Max replied, grabbing the needle with the red top. "That's fine with ME! The longer it takes for you to cooperate, the longer you WILL BE HERE, ANTONIO!"

"NO, NO, NOOOO! I'll chill. I'll relax."

"Good," Max sighed. "The sooner we get over this, the better it will be for all of us. I will give you something to eat after your bath if you are a good boy. I want this to relax you quickly so we can move on."

He reached for the bag of cotton balls on the tray and took two out. Next, he popped the top off the alcohol with his left hand, still gripping the cotton balls in his right. Placing the alcohol top on the tray, he then tilted the open bottle onto the cotton and rubbed my neck with the soaked cotton.

"Uuuuughhhhh!" he grumped with disgust. After scrubbing my neck, he stared at the cotton ball. "Look at this. Look at this filthy, filthy, dirty cotton!" Max placed the dirty cotton balls close to my eyes to show me his repulsion. "You're a filthy, filthy, dirty hood rat!"

What the fuck does he expect? I'm fucking dirty. I haven't fucking showered in a week.

Max moved my head over to the side forcefully and penetrated the needle through my flesh, squeezing the serum into my body. I could feel the warmth of whatever was in that needle oozing into my body. All I could think of was how much I hated needles and getting shots when I was a child. I remember running out of the clinic into the street when I was about to get a shot and almost getting hit by a car. My mom was upset but she didn't whoop me. I guessed she understood my fear.

My head slowly got warm and started to spin. I could feel my eyes getting heavy and low, almost to the point where they were closed. It was getting out of control. I could feel myself smiling really hard. It felt as if it was a big Kool-Aid smile from ear to ear. My body was hot and tingly. I couldn't hold my head up. It was a high that I have never felt before. I was on uncharted territory, but I was too high to be scared, I welcomed it.

"Yeaaah, you like that, don't you, Ms. Antonio?" Max asked.

I forgot where I was just that quick.

"How are you feeling? Are you ready for your bath? I don't want any mess from you, Antonio."

"I don't waaant any meeeesss from yoooou, Antoniooooo. Yoooou, you fucking maniac!" I said, trying to mock him, slurring just about my every word.

"I don't want any mess from you!" Max said once again. This time with sternness in his facial expression and voice.

"Mane, mane, maaaane, I'm cool," I said, trying to sound convincing. "I'm coooool. Reeeelax, my guuuy, I ain't gone start nooooo shit. But shiiiiit, speaking of shit, I have to shiiiiit real bad. I... I got the bubble guts, my guy. If you don't want me shitting on myself, I advise you to cut me loose because I got to shiiit reaaaal baaaad."

"You're already loose, dummy. You have been loose for 30 minutes. Your bath water is ready. Get your ass up," Max demanded.

"Ooooh, shit, well daaaamn Gina," I said still smiling and laughing at myself. I was sitting in the same chair and the ropes were gone. Glancing down, I realized I was free and butt ass naked. I looked down at my limp dick and played with it, flopping it with my hand.

"Stand up!" Max demanded a second time.

Shaking, I placed my hands on each side of the chair and attempted to push myself up. My legs started wobbling, as if they weren't going to support me and give out. I flopped back down in the chair. He reached down and grabbed me under my armpits, then slung me across his shoulder.

"Well, damn, Hercules, Hercules, Herculeeees!" I said, hearing my words slurring even more.

I began to laugh at myself. This mothafucka was so tall, big, and strong strong. All I felt was his muscles penetrating through his scrubs. He lifted me in both arms and used his foot to slowly nudge the bathroom door open. I didn't even have a chance to look around the place to see if anything looked familiar. It was too dark down in the corridor to make out anything. I believe the lights were intentionally off so that I wouldn't be able to see anything.

When we entered the bathroom, it felt very inviting. The lights were low, with scented candles burning. It was a tiny space with a small vanity and chair underneath it in front of a brass framed mirror. It was a small guest bathroom, that let me know that we were still downstairs in the basement; besides the fact that I didn't recall him climbing any stairs as he carried me. It smelled good, and it was heavily sanitized with bleach and Pine-Sol. *Man, I need to—*

Before I could finish my thoughts, Max said, "Sit your ass on the toilet!" He raised up the seat cover and centered me on the toilet. "Handle your business." He took a few steps back and leaned against that ugly ass flowered wallpaper. He crossed his arms and watched me, as if he was a prison guard.

"Man, I can't shit while you're in here and staring at me. What the fuck!"

"Well, you better try. And try really hard, Antonio, because I'm not leaving this bathroom! If you need some help, I have plenty of laxatives. If they do not work, I got a few more tricks that can help you get it out."

I shook my head and before I knew it, my bowels blurted out like diarrhea. I couldn't hold it in if I wanted to. It was horribly loud, disgusting, and very embarrassing. Suddenly, I was incredibly hot and sweat began pouring down my face as my stomach went into violent cramp convulsions. Feeling like I was going to pass out, all I wanted to do was lay on that cold tile floor and ball up in the fetus position. The only thing I could do was sit on the toilet, bend over, and try to get all of that built up waste out of me. The bathroom was abruptly filled with a fetid, putrid smell of what my stomach had been holding in for the last week. I don't know if it was the bowel movement or the stuff in that shot that he gave me, but I did know I was feeling a lot better and lighter. After about 20 more minutes, my stomach felt empty.

"Can you wipe your ass, or do I have to help you with that too?" Max asked.

"I... I can try and handle it myself, man."

"Good," he said, spraying air freshener around the bathroom and lighting more candles. "Now get up and get your nasty ass in the tub. I must sanitize this entire toilet."

"I... I can't, man, I'm woozy. My legs feel weak," I said, briefly standing up and sat back down.

"Come on," Max said, taking hold of me and helped walk me over to the tub. "Alright, put your left foot in first. Okay, now your right foot. I know it is warm, but you are a big boy, you can handle it."

The water was hot and silky from some type of bath oil that was in it. It was pleasantly pleasing to my worn-out body and mind.

"Now sit down."

Max threw a pink loofah bath sponge into the tub with me and handed me a bottle of body wash. It was MY body wash. It was my Eucalyptus Spearmint body wash. It was all MY shit that he took from my hotel room. The Eucalyptus Bath Fizzy that I was soaking in, the pink loofah bath sponge, and the damn body wash. So, he wasn't lying about going to my hotel room, but I hoped and prayed that he was lying about what he said about my mom.

"Humph," Max sighed, looking at me with disgust, bringing my attention to him and out of my head. "He is sooooo in love with you. For what? I just don't understand why." Shaking his head, he walked towards me with the chair from under the vanity and sat down next to the bathtub. He snatched the loofah out of my hand. "You don't even know how to bathe properly!"

Pouring my body wash onto the loofah, he began scrubbing my chest and stomach, then my arms and hands, following up with my neck and back. "You don't have your own place, and you don't even own a car. Stand up," he instructed me, standing up with me, with one hand under my armpit pulling me up. Squeezing more body wash onto the sponge, he began scrubbing my midsection, washing my dick and balls, then both of my legs, following up with my feet. "You don't have ANYTHING compared to me. You're not even that frickin cute, and my dick is far bigger than yours! Turn around!" Max began washing my back, cheeks, and down to my legs. "What the hell does he see in you? Now, you do have a nice ass, I must give you that." He said with slight disappointment in his voice.

"How he gone be MY partner, not let me penetrate him anymore, BUT then turn around and let you of all people crawl up his back? Bend your ass over so I can finish. I can't believe this!" With sorrow written all over his face, Max sat back down on the chair. "I legitimately cannot believe this." Holding his head down, he held it in his hands as his elbows rested on his legs. "All these years, all my frickin time and energy. It's okay, it's really okay because he's going to understand that you aren't crap. We can work it out, I forgive him. He just got caught up in YOUR shenanigans. He's going to see you for who you truly are!" Lifting his head up and looking at me with his forearms now resting on his legs. "Hurry up, Antonio, and rinse your ass off!"

Max's demeanor changed, and I didn't want to make it any worse. "I'm done. I'm done, sir!" I told him franticly. Out of being petrified, I didn't want him to get upset again. I have to play this shit out until I figure it out. How am I going to get the hell out of here? I don't know which lil shorty I was seeing that was involved with this crazy mothafucka. But I KNOW he ain't worth this shit. Fuck, none of them are.

"Come on get up," Max said, reaching down to help me stand up and step out of the tub onto the bathmat. He roughly dried me off, then aided me in putting on my robe and house shoes that I had left at the hotel. "Let's go." He commanded as we exited the bathroom and walked down the dark foyer.

Only a few steps — four or five — and to the left, we were in that ratchet weird ass room again. The mattresses still outlined the walls, and the strong stench of mildew was still thick. That broken lamp was still in the corner underneath the small boarded up window. The chair that I was once confined in sat there invoking fear into my heart next to a hospital bed in the center of the room — a twin bed with metal arm rails on both sides The remote dangled from the cord so you could lie flat or be forced upright. Druggy and all, I couldn't help but notice the arms and legs shackles attached to each side of the bed. Max stood me up, took the robe and slippers off me, then threw them on the chair. As he sat me on the bed, I could hear the plastic covering under the cool white sheets.

"Lay down," Max ordered.

"Please, please don't do this!" I pleaded with him while remaining sitting up. "I won't tell a soul." I promised him. "Just let me go, I won't see your dude anymore. I'll leave him alone. Sir, just let me go home, I pro—"

Before I could say another word. "SHUT THE HELL UP! YOU do not even know who he is, so how can you say you will leave him alone? He will never be ALONE anyway, because I will ALWAYS be here for him, even when he messes up!" Max said, pushing me down on the bed.

Aggressively grabbing my right arm, he attempted to lock it in the shackle. I swung at him with my tightly closed fist with all my might towards his head, hoping, wishing, praying that I would knock him the fuck out.

SWOOOOSH!

I missed. DAMN, DAMN, DAMN, I thought to myself.

"AAAAWWWW, you little prick!" Max yelled. "You're trying to swing on me, huh? You ungrateful little prick! I told you that you would regret doing something stupid!" He grabbed my throat with both hands, then began choking and shaking me.

I fought back trying to kick, bite, scratch, swing, and grab everything I could from his throat to his balls, all in a hopeful yet disappointing attempt.

Choking me even harder, he yelled, "You stupid prick, you stupid little PRICK!"

I couldn't breathe, I couldn't get a sound out, and I couldn't fight anymore. That was all I remembered of that night.

CHAPTER IV

Niggas and Flies

"Uuuuummmppphh, uuuggg!" I gagged.

Being blindfolded and retching was my newest wake-up call. I was violently shaking my head all around trying to get whatever was in my mouth out of it. It kept going deeper and deeper, reaching the back of my throat. I was going to throw up, I knew I was. The gagging was unmanageable. I couldn't see anything through the blindfold. My tears from the continuous dry heaving were leaking down my face through the cloth wrapped around my eyes. The shackles on my wrists and ankles were clinging and clanging as I struggled to get free. I was only hurting myself worse. Unexpectedly, my nose was being aggressively pinched with this thing stroking in and out my mouth! Aaaaahhh!!!! I can't breathe! I can't breathe!

My anger enraged me. Without another thought, I bit down as hard as I could on whatever it was until I felt my teeth grinding together. With my nose still being pinched, I couldn't taste what it was, but the texture was familiar. It was a cucumber, a fucking CUCUMBER! Using my tongue, I pushed out as much as I could as fast as I could to gasp for air to enter my lungs and breathe.

"Did you like that? Did you, Antonio?" Max asked as he snatched the blindfold off me. "I heard you were into sucking big things, so I thought you would enjoy a big, long French cucumber. I considered putting my dick in your mouth, but I kind of figured you were a biter. Damn, that French cucumber was at least a 14-incher! You were handling that like a pro. Well, until I pinched your nose. The next time it'll be something you can't clamp your jaws down on and spit out! I should have pegged you in the ass with it and then shoved it in and out of your mouth. By the way, this is going to be your meal for today. Eat while you can, because you're going to need your strength for later. Do you want me to slice it for you, or do you want to eat it whole?"

"I don't want that shit! I just want to get the hell up out of here! I want to go HOME!"

Looking around, I saw the cart with the silver tray on top of it, this time it had a white porcelain plate with two more huge ass cucumbers and a knife beside them. He picked up the plate and placed it on my leg. Holding the bed controller, Max pressed a button on it, sitting me up. He began slicing one of the cucumbers. Eating every slice he cut, he sat there tormenting me.

"Would you like a slice, Antonio?" Max asked, holding the knife with a slice of cucumber on it.

"I DON'T WANT THAT SHIT!" I yelled, turning my head away from him.

He snatched my face back towards him and looked at me as if I turned my nose up at a meal that he had prepared over a hot stove all day. As if I totally disrespected him. Max grabbed my nose and twisted it to the point where I couldn't breathe from my nostrils.

"WHAT THE FUCK! WHAT THE FUCK, MAX?!"

He picked up the other cucumber and shoved it in my mouth before I could scream another word. "EAT IT, EAT IT, YOU FUCKING PRICK! You're going to eat it, or I will force it down your fucking throat!" Max demanded. "You like sucking cock don't you, Antonio?! Pretend this is a big, long cock! You're going to eat it, Antonio, or I'm going to ram this motherfucker in your ass and then in your mouth!"

I started gaging again. Unable to breathe, I bit it. Max released his fingers from pinching my nose. He grabbed my head with one hand, gripped the bottom of my chin with the other, then slammed my mouth closed.

"Chew. Yeah that's it. Chew it, Antonio!"

I felt nauseous. Yet, I chewed and swallowed repeatedly, forcing every bite down my sorely inflamed throat. Feeling sick to my stomach, I wanted to throw up. It reminded me of the first time my mom made me eat beans and I threw up. She made me eat the rest of the beans from my plate even though I had thrown up and I was still gagging. I hated it, and I hated her for making me eat that shit. I never had a problem with cucumbers, but I hate them now more than beans, and I hate this monster more than anything!

"Well, Ms. Antonio, girl, you got some confessions to get off your chest today. Now, honey, what's the tea?" Max asked, trying to sound like one of my good friends.

It was pissing me the fuck off even more. He was sounding stupid and trying too hard to be funny. What a fucking loser! This mothafucka ain't no friend of mine.

"What's the tea about what, Max?" I asked him, annoyed as hell.

"You know, girl. Sooooo, who you been havin?"

"What, do you mean, 'who I've been havin?'"

"Girl, don't play with me. You know you done had a few guys that you have fucked around with in the last nine months," Max said, being sarcastic and mocking my friends.

"Max, I don't know what—"

SWAT!

"Oooohhh, SHIT!" I yelled out of surprise from being swatted in my face with that fucking nasty ass fly swatter.

SWAT, SWAT, SWAT, SWAT, SWAT, SWAT!

"Man, sto— sto— STOP! STOP!" I screamed and pleaded at every violent swat against my face, head, and neck with that fucking swatter. I could feel my face immediately beginning to welt up and swell.

"I don't like liars!" Max said with the same stern, ugly-ass face. His manner was no longer like my friends; it was back to the fucking raging lunatic that he really was. While reaching for the box of purple gloves, he rolled his eyes back towards me. "Don't play games with me, Antonio, and this doesn't have to get any more unpleasant for YOU!"

After putting the gloves on, Max snatched up the bag of cotton balls. Taking two out of the bag, he threw the bag back on the metal tray. He then took hold of the rubbing alcohol, opened it, and soaked the cotton balls. "I don't like liars, Antonio. I never did, and I never will. It's because of you that my fiancé has been lying to me. If it wasn't for you. . . you! You are just the typical greedy low life lying ass nigga. I was told a looong time ago, 'Nigga's and flies I do despise, because one eats shit and the other one tells lies!' YOU ARE A FUCKING LIAR, ANTONIO!" he yelled, pouring the rubbing alcohol out of the bottle directly over my inflamed head and face in his fit of anger.

"AAAAAHHHHH!!" I hollered in pain as the alcohol burned my face.

It felt like my skin was melting off! My face was on FIRE! My lips were swollen, my cheeks, my forehead, even on the right side of my neck I could feel the burn. Max then rubbed the alcohol-soaked cotton balls all over my face, harder and harder, ignoring my screams and begging for mercy. He didn't show me an ounce of compassion or sympathy.

This man truly despised and hated me. For what? I did not know. Max reached towards the tray and grabbed the needle with the orange top. Tilting my head, he punctured my skin once again full of serum. This time it was more inviting because I was in extreme discomfort, weak, and tired. As the warmth of the medication rushed to my head, I felt my head drop, and I began to drool on my bare chest. I tightly closed my eyes and streams of tears flowed down my cheeks.

"Open your eyes, Antonio, it's time to talk," he said as he slowly lifted my head up.

"No mooore please, nooo more. Please, Max, I'm sorry. I'm so sorry," I surrendered.

"Who have you been with this year, Antonio? Who have you had intercourse with? Where and when?" Max interrogated me, question after question. His voice sounded much more calmer and peaceful now that I was medicated. I was on cloud nine.

"Bro, I, I, don't knooooow. I've been with a feeeeew mothafuckas," I said. My head was swimming into deep blue oceans.

"I don't want to hear that, Antonio. I know you've been with a lot of people. I just want to know specifically about the ones in the last nine months or so!"

"I don't knoooow, Mister, I don't knoooow!! Maybe four or five. Maybe six or seveeeeen. I honestly don't remember!"

"DAMN IT! STOP TELLING ME YOU DON'T KNOW and REMEMBER!" he demanded, leaning over me holding the metal rails on the side of the bed with both hands.

I could hear the tension in his voice, but his voice was like a whisper. I didn't feel scared, intimidated, or anything. I just laid back with my eyes closed, feeling high and free, and tried to remember.

"Jerimiah, Jerimiaaaah!" I recounted.

"What about Jerimiah?" Max asked, walking away.

I turned my head to try to see if he was leaving. Stepping out of the room briefly, Max returned with another bottle of vodka in hand. He sat himself right back down next to me, as if he was an excited child awaiting to hear their favorite bedtime story. It frustrated me, but I didn't care. The drugs were doing its job. I just couldn't help but believe this perv was getting off on all of this and wouldn't let me go until he got what he wanted from me.

CHAPTER V

Going To School

"I... I met Jerimiah, well, I guess Jeri met me," I said, laying back trying to relax. "Max, this was waaaay longer than nine months ago. This was years ago. I was seventeen and a sophomore in high school when I met him. Jerimiah was about twenty-eight or twenty-nine back then. Sooooo, I know he ain't your dude!"

"Continue, ANTONIO!" Max demanded.

"FINE! I was walking to school with my little brother, and we were minding our own business as usual. I was mad and hated that it was so cold that morning. Our mom wasn't home that morning, and it wasn't shit in the house to eat. My day was already shitty as always!"

"Where was your father?" butted in.

"My father? Yeaaaah, okay my father was the typical sperm donor. He was a wanna be gangster, a wanna be drug dealer, and a wanna be pimp. BUT what he didn't wanna be was a fucking father! Just another nigga in the hood giving out community dick.

I had at least hoped for my mother's support and love but that was bullshit. All she wanted to do was run the streets, get high, and find her some peace of happiness outside of our fucked-up home!"

"Jerimiah, what about him?" Max stopped me before I could continue.

"Jeri drove his black-on-black Tesla next to the sidewalk that my little brother and I were walking to school on. He slowed down the momentum of his black rims to flow with every step we made. I could hear him bumping some old school shit through his cracked car windows, some Earth, Wind & Fire. Our mom used to play the same shit every Saturday afternoon when she would have us clean the apartment from top to bottom. This is when she wasn't out running the streets and felt she had some time to be around us."

"Go on with the story, Antonio," Max requested.

"Well, as soon as we stopped walking, the car stopped moving. The dark tinted window on the passenger side smoothly slid down. I took a quick glance to see who was driving. He was really cute from what I could see from the sidewalk.

"Hey, Pretty Red, y'all need a ride to school?" the driver asked, leaning over to the passenger seat.

"I knew what was up already."

"What do you mean?" Max asked with curiosity all in his voice.

"Max, the guy was trying to pick me up! He wasn't the first man that picked me up walking to school or walking anywhere. So, I knew what was up as soon as he started riding next to us."

"Did you let him?" Max asked.

"Yeah, yeah, I got in his car!"

As I told Max about what happened with Jerimiah, the memory hit me hard. I could feel the emotion rising before I even realized it. I knew that Jerimiah took advantage of me that morning. I allowed it because I was mad. I was mad that my mom wasn't home to cook breakfast for me and my little brother. I was mad that I was hungry and had to take another cold ass shower because the electricity was off again.

She knew my sister had to be at work before me and my brother even got up to go to school. That FUCKING BITCH! She was so selfish and inconsiderate! I was hungry and cold, and I hated going to that fucking school! Even though I knew Jerimiah was taking advantage of me, I felt that he could at least rescue me, even if it was just for a few hours or for the whole day.

"I told my lil brother to go straight to school and that I would meet up with him at the library after."

My brother looked at me, reluctant to walk away, and asked me, "Tony, do you know that man?"

"Yeah, Monty, I know him," I lied.

"Well, what's his name?" Monty asked, crossing his arms and waiting for my response, looking more feminine than me.

"I'm Jerimiah," Jerimiah answered Monty's question before I could think of another lie.

"Jerimiah? Jerimiah who, and why—"

Before Monty could ask Jerimiah anything else, I cut him off. Pushing him in the direction of the school.

"Monty, don't worry about all that. Take your ass to school, and I'll meet up with you later at the library." Monty still not moving much, I knew I had to promise him something. "Monty, after school we'll go get some pizza, and you can ride the go-carts at Incredible Pizza," I promised.

"Alright, Tony, you bet not be bull-shittin!" Monty said.

"Boy, watch your mouth, and take your ass to school. I got you when school is out," I promised him, opening the door to get into the car.

Looking at me holding my backpack on my lap, Jerimiah said, "You don't have to hold your backpack. You can place it on the back seat. I promise you; it'll be safe."

As I was leaning over the center console to place the backpack on the back floor, I heard Jerimiah say, "Mmm mmm."

My thongs were showing, I just knew it. I was wearing my cute pink Power Puff Girls crop top underneath my silver bubble jacket, and my low-rise gem stoned skinny jeans. My back and ass had to be out, I just knew it. My ass was phat and my waist was thin. I think I was a size 32 and about 130 pounds at that time. I was slim-thick. Being a track runner, everything I ate back then all seemed to go directly to my ass and legs. I got some of my ass and legs from my mother, and she got hers from my grandmother. That was one of the reasons why grown ass men were always fucking with me.

A lot of dudes my age would look but wouldn't really bite. They would just call me a punk and fag, and other stupid shit, but I knew what was up. When some of them would catch me alone it would always be a different story. They would corner me in the hallway when no one else was around and always grab and rub on my ass. Trying to tongue kiss me and asking me to give them head under the basketball bleachers after school. The only ones I would ever entertain were a few of the varsity football and basketball players. Some of them were even regulars, and all DL (Down Low) of course. They would call themselves dating cheerleaders but hit me up for head every week. The shit was laughable. Even the girls would grope my ass, and some of them were the girlfriends of the guys I was giving sloppy toppy to. That shit was laughable as well.

I was more of a dime piece than their girlfriends and most of the fish at that fucking school anyway. My body definitely had more curves than their bad weave, bad built, butch body asses. I was a Redbone with smooth skin — no blemishes, no bruises. My curls hung light brown and perfect around my shoulders, matching the warm honey in my eyes. Lips full and pink enough to make anybody stare twice. Flat stomach, thick thighs, and a phat ass that made the girls around me jealous without even trying. Those hoes had nothing on me. Their punk ass boyfriends couldn't do anything for me anyway. I was about my coins and grown men had it; high school boys didn't. Grown men also had grown men dicks, and I liked that a lot, but not more than I liked the coins that they gave me. I already knew if Jerimiah was trying to do anything with me, I was going to get some money out of him.

Now this is nice, I thought to myself as I turned back around, closed the door, and got settled in. *DAMN, it smells good up in here.* His car had that new car smell still lingering and he smelled good too. His Tesla was super clean and comfortable. Seeing him up front and personal, he was fine as all outdoors. Wavy natural red hair in a tight cut fade, red beard and mustache clean shaved and lined up, red skin with freckles, and green eyes. He was rocking a tight ass emerald-green Polo shirt so his green eyes could pop. His chest and biceps muscles would flex.

He wasn't fooling me, and I loved it. His Levi's 501 jeans and emerald-green retro Jordans let me know he was a little old school, as well as his music selection. It was a silent understanding between us, and basically any adult men I've dealt with — age wasn't up for discussion. What's understood, doesn't have to be explained. He reminded me of that singer Jidenna with his fine ass. It was just something about a black ginger that was so fucking hot and sexy to me.

"So, what's up, Pretty Red?" Jerimiah asked, reaching to shake my hand. Ooooohhh, his hand was so soft and well-manicured. "I'm Jerimiah, but you can call me Jeri." He had a deep and smooth voice. "What's your name?"

"I'm aaaahhh. . . Antonio."

"Well, Antonio, what do you wanna do?" he asked me with sooo much swag and confidence in his voice.

The way he was looking at me made me melt inside. "I... I'm down with whatever. You're the driver, so, so drive," I replied nervously. I hated it when I got nervous and stuttered.

"Well, we can go chill at my place if you want to."

"That's cool, we can do that. But I'm trying to get a few coins so I can take my brother somewhere after school, so he won't be snitching shit back to our moms," I responded promptly, trying to hide my diffidence.

"Shorty, you ain't got to be scared, relax. I'm not going to do anything to you that you don't want me to do. I won't bite, unless you say so. I'll drop some green in your pocket. If you want to just chill and watch tv, that's cool. If you want to get down on the PlayStation 5, that's cool too. Whatever you want to do is cool with me," Jerimiah said, seeing through my poor attempt to show any ounce of confidence.

He made me feel assured and safe, and I liked that. Reluctant to ask him, I asked anyway, "Mr. Jerimiah, if you don't mind me asking, where are you from?"

Flashing his gold teeth, Jerimiah smiled, and asked me, "Why, lil shorty? Where does it sound like I'm from?"

Hunching my shoulders, I looked at him. "I honestly don't know, sir. I do know you don't sound like you're from Memphis."

"Nah, lil shorty, I'm from NOLO," he answered, gleaming those pretty golds.

I didn't want to sound stupid, but I was curious to know, but before I could ask my next question, Jerimiah said, "Louisiana, lil shorty. New Orleans, Louisiana. I've been in Memphis for ten years. I guess I haven't lost my accent." He chuckled. "Did I answer your question?"

"Yeah, yes, sir, you answered it," I said, looking into his green eyes and smiling.

"Antonio, you don't have to call me sir. Jeri is just fine."

"I'm sorry," I said, patting his lap, trying to assure him that I was comfortable. Deep down inside, I was anxious as fuck. He was super fine. His swag was on point. His car was on point. Even his accent was on point! He was just my type. Like Saweetie said, "Rich, eight-figure, that's my type." I just wondered if he had that 8-inch good pipe. He probably doesn't. There are too many positive points for him NOT to have a small dick.

"There's nothing to be sorry for," Jeri said, interrupting my thoughts and rubbing my shoulder.

"Okay," I said as we rolled off.

Feeling a little better, I asked him to show me how to recline the seat. He pushed a button and my seat went back. Rubbing on my leg, he settled his hand on my upper thigh as I looked out of the window to daydream.

We arrived at his crib — damn, it was almost an hour's drive. I remembered seeing the time in his car when I hopped in around 7:30 a.m. When we arrived at his place, it was almost 9:00 a.m. I knew I had to have dozed off a few times because I didn't know where I was when I finally woke up. We were parked inside of a covered garage structure.

Rubbing my face with his delicate hand, Jerimiah said, "Wake up, sleepy head."

Hoping that I hadn't drooled on myself, I immediately pulled the visor mirror down to look at myself. "I'm woke."

When I got out of the car, I asked him where all the other cars were. He humbly told me that he owned the top floor condo with the attached garage, and that the Tahoe and BMW M440i xDrive Convertible were his also. I was absolutely impressed, but I did not want to show it. Jeri lived in a luxury high-rise condo on the top floor. I could see myself living there, *shit I wish*. With Jeri holding my hand, we walked from his car into the double doors that led inside into his kitchen. He made me feel like fish holding my hand. I wanted to be his little princess. He was about 6'2" to my 5'5".

"Would you like something to drink?" Jeri asked, standing in the kitchen.

"Yes, please."

"What would you like?" Jerimiah asked, opening the refrigerator doors.

I couldn't help but think, *damn his fridge is like a fucking grocery store.* It was bright to the point of almost being blinding, and it was very well systematic. He had a variety of everything I could think of to drink: milk, juices, smoothies, teas, and a lot of different water bottles.

"Bottled water is cool," I said, not wanting to seem desperate.

"Which one because there are several different brands to choose from."

"Shit, just give me any one of em, as long as it's cold, I'll be okay."

He popped the top off a bottle of S.Pellegrino and poured it into a small glass. "Do you want ice in it?"

"No, thank you, Jeri," I said, looking up at him into his beautiful eyes. "It's cold enough."

I couldn't help but think, *this nigga was too damn fancy for my ghetto ass.* Holding my hand again, we walked into the living room.

"Have a seat," he said, turning the television on.

"Thank you."

"Do you want something to eat?" Jerimiah asked.

"No, sir, I'm good right now." I was already on an empty stomach, so I didn't want to eat anything anyway. Especially if he was going to fuck me, which I knew he would do eventually.

"Stop calling me sir," Jerimiah said, softly looking into my eyes.

"My bad. I'm going to remember, Jeri."

He sat next to me on the sofa. He rubbed my leg and just started staring at me.

I looked at him, and asked him, "What are you staring at?"

"I'm staring at you, beautiful." He leaned towards me and kissed me.

His lips were so soft, and his tongue was sweet. I wanted to chew it like bubble gum. I settled for sucking on it instead. I guess that prompted him to suck on my tongue also.

Suddenly, he stopped and sat back. "Stick out your tongue," he instructed.

I stuck it out, showing him the two piercings I had in it. I touched the center of my nose with my tongue and then the bottom of my chin.

He looked at me with a single raised eyebrow, like how the Rock does. Smiling he said, "Damn, Pretty Red, that's some sexy ass shit."

I started blushing. His whole vibe had me at hello. He gently grabbed my face with both of his hands and pulled me to his lips. We kissed so passionately it made me hot. I struggled to take my jacket off while continuing to kiss him without missing a beat. As we kissed, I played in his beard, and his hand went underneath my shirt to rub my pointed nipples and lightly pinched them. With one hand caressing my chest and nipples, he used his other hand to rub my back.

Jeri's hand on my back went down to my waist. From my waist it went to the center lower part of my back. He pulled on the back of my thongs and started twirling it with his fingers. Out of curiosity, I decided to utilize my other hand to explore since he was using his to explore. Feeling a little nervous, I boldly began rubbing on his leg until I reached the area that I was really curious about exploring. I always play shy. During my rubbing exploration, I came across a rather large, long lump in his jeans in between his legs. I couldn't take a look at it because I didn't want to take my tongue out of his mouth or him to take his out of mine. What I could only conclude was that this nigga was carrying a baby anaconda in his jeans.

Playfully, I poked it a few times. He made that big motherfucker jump, and I jumped too. Jeri started laughing while still tonguing me down. Smiling, I asked, "What are you laughing at, Jeri?"

"At your sexy ass, Pretty Red. Did Big Willie scare you?" Jerimiah asked, still trying to kiss me.

"Hell, yeah, it scared me. What are you packing in those jeans?"

Still trying to suck on my tongue, he mumbled, "12."

Pushing him off me, I asked him, "What did you say?"

Pulling me by my waist, bringing me back to him, he kept kissing me. "12."

I pushed him off me with both of my hands on his chest, holding him back from trying to kiss me anymore. Looking into his eyes, I asked him for the third time, "Jerimiah, how big is your dick?"

Looking at me just as seriously as I was looking at him, he answered, "Lil shorty, it's 12-inches. It's long and thick. Bitches can't handle it. Some dudes do but some never come back for seconds. I was hoping you could. Is there a problem?" Jerimiah asked with all sincerity in his voice and eyes.

I have been with some men with some pretty big dicks. I have never been with a man that had a dick like Jerimiah's, and I haven't even seen it yet. I only felt it and saw its print through his pants. *Damn.* I knew he would fuck me good. I knew he would take good care of me and be gentle because he seemed to be a gentle giant. Even with thinking about all of that, I couldn't help but ask myself, *could I handle it?* I definitely wanted to try. I wanted to try so badly. My stomach was empty, so I knew that I wouldn't paint him. This dude was on point, and he just captivated me. He leaned in to continue our kissing.

As much as I wanted him to rip off our clothes, I pushed him back, and said, "I thought we were going to watch television."

He sat back on the sofa. "My bad, lil shorty. Alexia, play porn on living room tv.

I took a sip of my water, thinking *damn* to myself. Those other lame ass fuckers before didn't have shit on Jeri. Those mothafuckas never offered me to come chill at their crib. They never even offered me a drink of water. Those perverts just wanted me to suck their dicks or suck mine while they jacked off in their broke down ass cars in dark allies, behind Burger King, or under the freeway. They would give me a few dollars and catch up with me in a month or so to do the same dull shit all over. I grabbed my glass of water and walked over to the window.

Jerimiah's living room window stretched from one end of the wall clear to the other. It was huge and had a view of the entire city. I was still uncertain where we were, but I loved it.

Turning to Jeri as he sat on the sofa watching some nasty ass hetero porn, I told him, "I'm willing to try, but I'm scared that it's too big, and it's going to hurt too much."

Jeri smiled, got up, and joined me at the window. Upon approaching me, he grabbed my waist with both of his hands and pulled me closer to him. Looking into my eyes, he said, "Lil shorty, I'll take good care of you. If you tell me to stop, I'll stop. I want you to enjoy it just as much as I do."

That made me feel a tad bit more at ease. He lifted my head up and kissed me softly on my lips. He told me that he had something that would help me relax. Jeri went into the kitchen while I stood there looking out of the window. Daydreaming and wondering why my parents couldn't achieve the things that Jeri had achieved. He returned to me at the window and gave me a glass of what looked like sweet tea with some ice cubes. Taking away my glass of water, he told me to drink what was in the glass he handed to me. I wondered how sweet tea was going to help me relax if it's full of caffeine.

I said, "Okay." I proceeded to drink it as if it was sweet tea. It was so strong it burnt my throat, and I started coughing.

"No, no," Jeri said faintly. "Take it slow. That's not something you gulp down."

Shaking my head. "What is it?"

Jerimiah explained, "It's brandy, you have to sip on it. It's really smooth, but you can't just gulp it."

"Ooooh, okay," I responded, looking at him slightly embarrassed.

"There's nothing to be embarrassed about, baby," Jeri comforted me as he held me next to him. He placed both of his silky soft hands down my back, reaching both of my ass cheeks inside my jeans.

"Ooooo, your hands are cold," I told him with a little shiver in my voice.

"My bad, shorty, I forgot I just made our drinks."

"It's okay, it felt good, it just surprised me. Put them back, Jerimiah."

He did as I wished and placed both of his hands back in my jeans, holding onto my cheeks. "Damn, baby, you got some cakes back here, a couple of basketballs," Jerimiah said, smiling like he was already imagining trouble.

I looked up at him, and told him, "I know, I've been told. All natural, no BBL's here, baby.

His hands clutched my derriere, making it bounce beneath his grip. Then he dipped down and kissed me — slow, deep, full-on French for five minutes.

"Take off your jeans so I can see exactly what you got from my mama," he requested.

"I'll take mine off if you take yours off," I countered offered.

Jeri said, "Say less." He took off his shoes and kicked them to the side.

After taking off his shirt, he threw it on top of his shoes. What a beautiful specimen of a man he was with freckles all over his chest and six-pack. I could tell for sure that he spent a good amount of time in the gym and that he took pride in his body. He began unbuckling his belt, gazing at me as if he was challenging me. I started sliding my jeans down, keeping an eye on him because I wanted to see his package. I knew my eyes probably looked like they were bulging out of my eye sockets, but I couldn't help it. His shit looked like it was inches away from his knees and it wasn't even hard. My stomach suddenly was filled with butterflies.

It was long, thick, and uncut! His pubs were just as bright red as the hair on his head and face. I was surely in uncharted territory. I had never been with a ginger or a guy with such a huge snake, and I'd never been with a guy that was uncut.

Jeri just smiled at me again, flashing his gold grills. "It's more of a shower. Not too much of a grower, but trust and believe it gets nice and hard."

Pulling his foreskin back exposing his massive, freckled mushroom head, he started slapping his dick into his hand. *WACK, WACK, WACK.* Hearing how heavy his meat sounded, smacking in his hand made me feel a bit cautious, but I wasn't a punk. I wasn't about to punk out. I took a swallow from my glass and placed it on the window seal. After taking my boots off, I placed them on the floor next to his shoes. Once my jeans were off, I slid them to the side with my foot.

"I could tell your dick was long and hard when I was poking it while we were on the couch."

Jeri looked at me. "DAMN, baby, you are slim thick for real. Turn around and show off what you're working with for daddy."

Again, he had me blushing. I slowly turned around for him, modeling my little pink Power Puff Girls crop top and pink thongs. Back facing him, he smiled at me doing that eyebrow thing again and turned me back around.

When my backside was facing him, Jeri said, "SHIT, lil baby, stay just like that." He pulled my thongs down.

While massaging my booty, he kept telling me how soft it was and how it was shaped better than most of the women he fucked around with. After massaging it for a few minutes, he bent me over. I stepped out of my thongs and moved them to the side with my foot. There I stood with only my crop top on bending over, touching my toes. Jeri got on his knees and spread my legs open. Using both of his hands, he opened my ass cheeks and started licking and sucking on my clean-shaven hole and all around it. Again, I was in uncharted territory because I had never had my ass eaten. It was always me giving blow jobs, me getting a blow job, or me just getting fucked.

Jerimiah's tongue was so warm, wet, and welcoming. It felt so damn good. He stuck his tongue deep inside of me. He began wiggling it and stroking it in and out. I was really feeling like fish, moaning and all. I reached around and grabbed his head with both of my hands and pressed his face as much as I could deep between my cheeks so that he could get his tongue as deep as he possibly could inside of me. Backing up off me after a few minutes, Jeri told me to get down on my hands and knees, and I did.

"May I have another drink, Jeri?"

"Come here," he said, still on his knees.

On my knees, I scooted closer to him. "Yes, daddy?"

"Baby, you can have whatever you want."

"May I have a kiss then?" I asked him while smiling.

Leaning towards me, Jeri grabbed my head with both of his hands and sweetly tongue kissed me. I grabbed his dick just to hold that beast in my petite hands while we kissed. He moaned, and I moaned as our tongues feverishly wrestled.

"I want to taste Big Willie."

"What about your drink?"

"You can get it after I taste you.

"Say less," Jeri said, slapping his dick on his hand.

"Lay on your back please."

Jeri complied with my request. Crouching over him with my ass inches from his face, I proceeded to make love to his penis with my mouth. He vigorously rubbed my booty with both of his hands in a circular motion. Already knowing I wouldn't be able to deep throat all of Big Willie, I decided to focus on the head of the beast. Even this nigga's dick smelled and tasted good. His pubs smelled good as well. I wanted to deep throat his dick all the way down to his pubs and balls so bad, but I kept gagging. While I was doing my best to please him, he spread my cheeks and began to please me. Minutes later, he told me to sit up on his face.

I did as he urged, still holding and stroking Big Willie with both of my tiny hands. Jeri had my ass spread wide open and had it soaking wet from his hot salvia. I guess this was a better position for him to work by reason of he was putting in some marvelous work. I couldn't help but shriek with ecstasy as long as he had my cheeks wide open and his tongue was all up in my hole.

"Jerimiah, JERI!" I silently squealed out.

He didn't stop to answer me, and I really didn't want him to. The more I called his name, the more aggressively he sucked, licked, and stroked my hole with his tongue. I felt so amazingly sexy and turned on. Letting go of his dick, I started pinching both of my nipples and rubbing my ass while riding the fuck out of his face.

"JERI, JERI, YOU'RE GOING TO MAKE ME CUM!" I yelled

I couldn't believe it. How the hell could this nigga make me nutt just by eating my ass? Neither of us were touching my dick, so how could this even be possible? However, he was doing it. He was doing it, and I didn't care how anymore. I just rode his face harder, and he ate me more vigorously.

"JERI, I'M CUMMING!" I shouted!

Jeri didn't mind me, he just kept having his all you can eat buffet. His strong hands holding my cheeks open, his tongue in and out of my hole, feeling his drenched mustache and beard moving all around my hairless ass. My dick and balls were bouncing up and down on his chin and neck. I was grinding my tight, sopping, wet orifice all over his face. I couldn't hold it back, and I didn't want to hold it back. My ass started clinching up but Jeri and I both held it open. My nutt sacks began to tighten and release what I didn't want to hold back any longer. My dick stiffened and was standing straight up! Before I knew it . . .

SKEEEEEET, SKEEEET, SKEEET

"JERIIIIIIII!"

My nutt shot out fast and furious, all the way past his feet and was still shooting! He was still eating my ass, and I continued to nutt all over myself and him. That shit felt so fucking deviously delicious! My body was just shaking and shaking. I couldn't believe it. It was surreal, and I loved every bit of it. Jeri lifted me up to his chest after he was done lavishly devouring my spittle-soaked anus.

"Pretty Red, did you enjoy that?"

I turned around, straddling his midsection, and asked him, "What the fuck do you think?"

Leaning down towards his sweet dripping lips, we kissed. It was so fucking hot, and it turned me all the way on! I loved the way that nigga kissed me! Rubbing on his facial hair while he kissed me turned me on even more! He was so masculine and rugged, but gentle and sweet. I haven't even had the dick yet and this nigga made me cum just by eating my ass, I can only imagine what that dick does. I was still intimidated by the size of it, but I wasn't going to not at least try that motherfucka out. This nigga was fire; he was everything that I wanted in a man! I stood up over him holding his hands.

"What now, Jerimiah?"

"I'm going to go fix you that drink now." He grabbed our glasses from the window seal.

"Thank you, baby," I said, watching him walk towards the kitchen.

Jeri had a cute, dinky, flat booty with freckles all over it. It jiggled as he walked. What he lacked in ass, he absolutely made up for it with dick, that's for damn sure. I turned from watching him and started to gaze out of that magnificent window again. My body was still in shock from that strong ass orgasm, so my legs were still shaking a little. Jeri walked up behind me and gently placed his hands on my chest underneath my crop top. He startled me, and I think he knew it because he pulled me closer to him. I could feel his dick pressing against me as well as the heat from his body. He felt good and soothing.

We both just quietly stood there while he held me, looking out of the window admiring the view. Part of me, well, a great deal of me didn't want the moment to slip away. I had just met Jerimiah that morning and in our short time together, he made me feel so many emotions. No longer was I angry about how my morning started off. No longer was I pissed off at my mother. None of that shit mattered anymore. The only thing that mattered at that moment was Jerimiah holding me and us looking out of that window enjoying the view together. I wanted him to be mine, and I wanted him to want me to be his. I didn't want to go back home to all the chaos and damn drama. It was quiet here. I wanted that, I needed that, and I most certainly loved that.

Kissing me on my neck, Jeri said, "Let's go to my bedroom, lil baby."

"Sure thing, daddy." Remembering, I asked him, "What about my drink?"

Jeri assured me that everything was in his bedroom. He picked me up, as if I was his bride. I wrapped my arms around his neck, laid my head against his chest, and went with the flow. He walked down the hallway carrying me. He told Alexia to turn off the television and the lights in the kitchen and living room. Entering his bedroom was like entering a fancy hotel room. I mean a really grand hotel suite. It reminded me of the extravagant suite at the Beverly Wilshire Hotel that was in the movie, 'Pretty Woman'. It was massive.

He had the largest bed that I've ever seen in my life with a black leather headboard that was centimeters from the ceiling. There was a black leather recliner with a matching sofa and a coffee table. He had two candles burning on each end of his nine-drawer black marble dresser with a 60-inch mirror. There also was a black marble nightstand on both sides of the bed with lit candles. The aromatics were divine, arousing, and calming. I couldn't tell how big the window was because he had black, black-out curtains covering them, but it was wall to wall like the window in his living room.

"Alexia, turn off room 1 lights, turn on blue LED lights, play Prince Rogers slow jams." He closed the bedroom door.

Walking me to the bed, he softly placed me on it. He took my shirt off, placed it on the nightstand, then kissed me on my forehead. Standing butt ass naked right in front of me with his big ass ding-a-ling just hanging, he took our glasses off the nightstand and handed me mine. Picking up two blue pills off the nightstand, he handed me one and took the other one following it with a sip from his glass.

"What is it, Jeri?"

"It's a Percocet, lil shorty."

Not wanting to sound dumb, but I asked him, "What it was for?"

"It relieves pain, and it will bring you to a state of euphoria."

"But I'm not in any pain," I said, looking and feeling confused.

"I know, baby, but this will ensure that you don't be in any pain during and after."

"Ooooooh, I understand, I get it." I giggled as I took the pill and took a drink from my glass. Looking up at him from sitting on the bed, I asked him, "What now?"

"It'll take 15 to 30 minutes to kick in. It'll reach its peak in about an hour and last about three hours. So, it's up to you."

"Well, I know what I can do until it kicks in," I said enthusiastically.

"Now, what would that be, Pretty Red?" Jeri asked, looking down at me with one eyebrow raised.

Without saying another word, I grabbed his manhood with both of my hands and rubbed down his shaft so that his foreskin came down so that big, freckled mushroom head would come out. I began to satisfy him orally. Stretching my mouth open as much as I could, I still could only get so much of that anaconda in it. I wanted desperately for it to touch the little jiggly thing in the back of my throat, my tonsils. The challenge was on because he wasn't even hard yet. With as much of it as I could fit in my mouth, I began to tongue kiss the head of his dick, making sure he slightly felt my tongue piercings. While doing so, I massaged his shaft with both of my hands up and down.

I knew he was starting to enjoy it because of his moans, but mainly I knew because his dick started hardening. It was now my time to shine and show off. With my head going back and forth with great vigor on his head and pole, I continued stroking his shaft with one hand. I began to cuff, gently squeeze, and massage his fat, full, freckled balls. I could taste his sweet precum in my mouth and that made my mouth water more. My saliva was pouring out of my mouth down my neck to my chest, and down his pikestaff to his balls.

At that point, Jeri's moans grew louder and louder. He grabbed my head with both of his hands and began to thrust his meat deeper into my salvia filled lubricated mouth, finally reaching that little jiggly thing in the back of my throat. My eyes started to water, and I started gagging but I didn't want to stop. I wanted him to shoot all his hot load into my mouth and fill it up so I could swallow every drop of it.

He stopped me. "DAAAMN, Pretty Red, you got a hella hot mouth on you." He grabbed me by my throat with one hand as I looked up at him as pure and innocently as I could. "Open your mouth," Jeri instructed.

I did as he wished. Jeri took a swallow from his glass and leaned down towards me. He poured the brandy into my mouth from his mouth. *DAMN,* I thought to myself. That shit was fucking sexy ass fuck.

"Has that perk kicked in yet?" he asked me, rubbing my face.

"I think so, daddy. I'm feeling really gooood and horny."

"Good shit," he said. "Cause I'm about to put this dick all up in your guts."

Just him saying that and talking to me like that made my dick hard and my hole wet. I knew he was going to do exactly what he said he was going to do, and I was ready for him and Big Willie to fuck the dog shit out of me anyway he wanted. I was his for the taking.

"Scoot over to the center of the bed, baby," Jeri said after he took a sip from his glass.

Lying on the center of the bed on my stomach with my legs bent and feet in the air, I just couldn't help but stare at him because he was so handsomely beautiful. After grabbing something out of the nightstand drawer, Jeri got up on the bed with me. I laid in the middle of that giant bed feeling so comfortable and relaxed, just awaiting him to touch me. Lying next to me on his side, he placed a couple of Maximum condoms and a small black bottle of what I believe was lubricant next to one of the pillows behind me. He started rubbing on my ass like I knew he would. That's why I was on my stomach.

"Are you ready?" Jeri asked.

"Yes, baby, I'm ready. I'm on cloud nine, and I feel truly genuinely placid. I'm ready for you if you are ready for me," I said, stroking his face and beard.

Turning me over onto my back, Jeri moved closer to me, and we began to French kiss. As our kissing got deeper and more intense, we wound up on our sides holding one another, chest to chest, stomach to stomach, and dick to dick. I tightly wrapped my arms around his neck and Jeri wrapped his arms around my waist. Grinding our bodies against each other, I propped one of my legs over his. Laying me back on my back, Jeri got on top of me and started sucking on my neck and we started frotting. I wrapped my arms and legs around him as he continued to rub his 12-inch penis against my 8-inch penis. I could feel the wetness of precum between us, but I wasn't sure if it was his, mine, or the both of ours.

I didn't care either, it was a sticky situation that I openly greeted. The shining blue LED lights, the heat of our bodies pressing against each other, the alcohol, the Percocet, the ambiance, the tranquility of the tantalizing aroma of the candles, all of it made me want to explode right then and there. Jeri moved from sucking on my neck to sucking on my nipples. Opening my legs with both of his hands, he went down to my navel, licking it and playing with my belly ring with his tongue. I laid there gripping his head with my legs open for his taking. Lifting my legs up over both his shoulders and palming my ass cheeks in both of his hands, Jeri began licking and sucking on my asshole and all around it.

Still holding on to his head, I began to weep with pleasure. When he stuck his tongue deep inside of my aperture, I thought that I was going to lose it! Gently laying me back down on the bed, Jeri reached over me and grabbed the lube. He kneeled in front of me as I laid there hot, bothered, and ready. He opened the lube and poured some in his hand. Rubbing the lube on and around my tight starving anus, Jeri slowly inserted his large, thick index finger inside of me.

"Oooohh," I sighed.

"Relax, baby, I got you. I just want to open you up a little," Jeri said as he did exactly what he said he wanted to do.

Unhurriedly and mildly in and out of my ass, he slid his lubricated finger. Once he felt my tensed hole loosening up, he inserted two of his fingers in and out of me. Jeri knew I was ready for more when I began to murmur with relief and moved my hole in a way to take in more inches of his fingers. Reaching behind me, he grabbed a condom while continuing to fuck me with his two long, meaty fingers. I've seen Maximum condoms before, but I had never seen Maximum XXL condoms. Jeri's dick was rock hard and standing at attention, and I wanted to give it its attention. He poured lube onto his hand and massaged some on Big Willie.

Tearing the condom open, he tossed the wrapper to the side of the bed. Pulling his foreskin back, he placed the condom over his fat mushroom head and down his thick anaconda. The condom barely went completely down his entire shaft. Rubbing lube on his sheathed dick and more lube on my hole, he opened my legs, hovered over me, and began to insert himself into me.

"OOOOHH!" I gasped and grabbed his shoulders as just the head of his penis broke the threshold of my slippery lubricated hole.

"You good, baby?" Jeri asked, leaning in closer to me.

"Yeah. Yes, I'm good, baby.

Without hurry or delay, Jeri entered me crescively, filling me and stretching me open as Big Willie made his grand entrance into my welcoming, warm, throbbing hole. As I said before, I've had some big dicks in my life before, but nothing like Jeri's. I grabbed his waist and opened my legs more to accept him. That and my moans of pleasure gave him the green light to go deeper. Taking the hint like the smart man that he was, Jeri went deeper.

"AAAHHH," I whimpered, moving my hands from his waist to his chest as he filled himself all the way inside of me.

Placing his hands underneath my shoulders and holding them, Jeri started slowly thrusting his dick back and forward inside of me, bringing the tip of his dick to the opening of my hole but not pulling it out of me.

"You good, baby?" Jeri asked.

"YES, JERI, YES!!"

Jeri's strokes picked up momentum and went deeper, my legs opened wider as we became rhythmically instinct. Pressing his body closer to mine while holding me tightly to him, we started kissing passionately. Not only were our bodies now rhythmically in sync, our moans and groans became harmonized as we made stimulating love to one another.

"You like this DICK, don't cha, lil shorty?! Don't cha?!" Jeri asked.

"YES, JERIII, YES! DON'T STOP FUCKING ME, DADDY!"

Sitting up while still fucking me, Jeri grabbed my foot and started sucking on my toes! He grabbed my other foot while his dick was still putting in work on my hole and started taking turns sucking on my toes from each foot. Once again, I was in uncharted territory, and I loved it there. Jeri's strokes became deep with purpose and were intentionally entering my central zone, hitting my G-spot, my prostate.

"AAAHHH, JERIIII, OOOOHH, YEESS, YEESS, FUCK ME, DADDY! OOOOHH MAKE ME CUM! I CAN FEEL IT, BABY! I CAN FEEL IT!" I exclaimed.

"I can feel it too, lil baby! OOOHH, YEEAAHH! I can feel it, baby! Give daddy that boy pussy! GIVE IT TO ME!"

"TAKE IT, JERI! AAAHHH TAKE IT, BABY! OOOOHH, YAASSS, DADDY!"

Extending far down into me, I tightly held on to Jeri as Big 12-inch Willie pummeled my prostate. I was cumming once again without my dick being touch! I was cumming hard!

"OOOOHH, SHIIIT, JERI, I'M CUMMIN, I'M CUMMIN, BABY!"

"I'M CUMMING TOO, LIL SHORTY! I'M CUMMING TOO! YOUR ASS IS SOOOO TIGHT AND HOT! IT'S SOOOO GOOOD, BABY!"

"OOOOHH, YES, DADDY, YAASSS! FUCKING CUM WITH ME! CUM WITH ME! BUST THAT SHIT, DADDY! AAAHHH! YES, FUUUUCK, YES, YES, YEEEESSS!"

The more I felt my orgasm coming, the tighter my hole compressed Jeri's dick. The closer Jeri got to his orgasm, the more solid and hard his dick got! It was time. Securely holding on to one another, our bodies sensuously danced as the sweat from our bodies mixed into an ocean of intoxicating pheromones. With no desire to hold back, we allowed our genitalia to do what comes naturally. Jeri and I simultaneously came together into a state of fierce euphoria.

"AAAAAAAHHH!" we both moaned and exhaled.

Jeri fell to my side lying on his back and grabbed me into his arm. I turned on my side and laid my head on his hot sweaty chest and reached up to rub his beard. He took hold of my ass cheek, palmed it, and started tongue kissing me. We laid there together in our nakedness, holding one another silently trying to catch our breath.

CHAPTER VI

A Stranger In The House

"Jerimiah liked me and he was definitely into me. I fell in love with him, and I was absolutely head over heels. The way we started off was subconsciously a bother for me, because I felt like I was nothing more than his sneaky link, some lil fresh ass he picked up on the streets."

"So, did you continue to see Jerimiah?" Max asked.

"Yes, yes, I did, and I still do. I was just with him before I flew to Atlanta. I'm tired of talking. I'm thirsty and hungry. Jeri wasn't your fiancé so why am I still talking about him. You DON'T KNOW HIM!"

"Antonio, you would be surprised by *WHO* I know," Max responded with a crooked smile. "But you are right, I don't know Jerimiah. But I DO KNOW ABOUT HIM! I know all about him through your conversations with my fiancé. I know the both of you had a threesome with Jerimiah. I know you still fuck with the both of them and a few others, that is THAT! I want you to UNDERSTAND everything you discussed with my baby, I KNOW ABOUT IT! Your story about Jerimiah checks out, I see no lies told by you on that. Let's keep it that way, Antonio, and we can get through this. Who was next in your last nine months of escapades?"

Laying there, I was angrier because this monster knew so much about my damn business. The shit was annoying as fuck. Who the fuck did he get all this tea from about me? Who the hell is his fiancé? "Can I get something to drink or eat first? Can I use the bathroom? Max, what the fuck? Just tell me who the fuck your boyfriend is! I'll tell you what you want to hear! My face is hurting and bleeding! I'm tired! I want to go home! I'm SICK OF THIS SHIT! JUST TELL ME WHO YOUR BOYFRIEND IS, MAX!"

"He's my FIANCÉ DAMMIT! NOT MY BOYFRIEND! HE'S NOT MY BOYFRIEND, ANTONIO! And NO, Antonio, you're NOT going to tell me what I want to hear! You, my friend, you are going to tell me the TRUTH, THE WHOLE TRUTH, AND NOTHING BUT THE TRUTH before I give you ANYTHING!"

Max yanked a pair of gloves from the box on the cart and slipped them on. He grabbed a handful of cotton balls, then picked up the needle with the orange cap and tapped it a few times with his thumb.

"NOOO, NOO, I don't want it! Please, Max! Please, sir!" I cried out, tears pouring down my face, stinging every open wound as I begged him to stop.

"This is going to make you feel better, Antonio. It's going to help you relax and calm down. Lifting my arm up, Max rubbed the alcohol-soaked cotton balls on my forearm. I felt he showed me some piece of compassion by not rubbing the alcohol on my bruised neck. After flicking the syringe to get the air bubbles out, he inserted it into my arm. It didn't take long for the drug to enter my empty system. My head swam, my stomach cramped, and I felt my eyes rolling up to the top of my head. The only thing I heard was low pitch humming as everything became darkness.

"Wake up. Come on, wake your ass up, Antonio!"

"Wha... Wha... What? What's going on? What's going on?" I asked dazed and confused. I was conscious, but drugged so much I couldn't see straight, let alone gather my thoughts. His horrifying voice drew me back into the very nightmare that I prayed that I had escaped. I was still shackled down in the hospital bed. I was still hungry and thirsty. It was some straight bullshit. I guess I dozed off for a minute. "How... how long did I doze off for?" I could hear my words slurring.

"Two days!" Max responded with an aggravated tone in his voice. "You wouldn't wake up. I may have given you too much Barbiturate. Next time, I must make sure I change your dosage because I can't get what I want out of you if you keep falling into a coma."

"Two days? Are you fucking kidding me, Max! What the fuck man! Max, why... why are you keeping me here? What are you going to... to... doooo to me? I need to go home, Max! Please let me go! I have to go back to work. My family and friends are probably losing their minds wondering where the fuck I am!"

"Your family and so-called friends are just fine, Antonio. You told them that we are vacationing in the Caribbeans. They sent their love and told us to be safe. So, there is no need for you to concern yourself about your family, friends, your home, your job, or anything else! I want you to CONCERN yourself with getting down to the truth of why you wound up here! As soon as I am satisfied with what I want to know from you, you will be able to go about your merry way, Antonio."

Max continued, "I wanted to be done with this last night, but you became unresponsive, and I wasn't able to finish ANYTHING! You are wasting too much of my time! Let's get to the TRUTH, and we can get this over with! Now, that I've cleaned your nasty ass again, and you are awake, you can have something to eat before we talk." He turned his head, looking at the door. "Hold on, I'll be right back!"

Max hurriedly walked out of the room, leaving the door cracked open. I could hear him conversing with someone down the corridor. I could hear someone talking WITH him. Somebody is in this house with this psycho. Somebody is here!

Without another thought, I screamed, "HEEELLLPPP! I'VE BEEN KIDNAPPED! I'M IN HERE, I'M IN HERE! HELP ME! PLEASE SOMEBODY, HELP ME!" I hollered as loud as my hoarse voice would allow.

The voices stopped. There was only silence for the next few minutes that seemed as if it were hours. I heard footsteps with keys jiggling running towards the door. The door slammed closed and was locked. They were arguing. Trying to hear their words was hard for me to do. I tried to make sense of the utterance that came down the hallway through the door that imprisoned me. The voices moved away and drifted until I heard nothing.

"COME BACK! PLEASE COME BACK! I'M IN HERE! I'M ANTONIO! PLEASE HELP ME! PLEASE SOMEBODY HELP MEEEE!

Whoever it was had heard me. They had to hear me. They're going to rescue me or get help for me. I'm sure someone must have heard me because that maniac heard me and came running back, slamming the door closed. So, I know whoever he was talking to had to hear me also. This shit is over, it's finally over. I'm going to go home. I'm going to see my mama and my little brother. I'm going back to work. No more bullshit, no more being late, no more calling off. I'm going to get my shit in order. I'm going to find a partner and settle down, and it's going be me and him.

No more fucking around with all these punks; that shit is too much drama. I'm going to find me a little piece and settle my ass down. That's what I'm going to do. If Jerimiah doesn't want to settle down with me, the hell with him. I'm finished with this shit. I'm done. I'm DONE! I promise to God, I am DONE!

Seconds turned into minutes and minutes turned into hours. I lay there in complete quietness, struggling to stay awake, to stay hopeful, and to stay positive. I felt myself nodding off as my head kept falling. Every time, I caught myself. I would wake up with less and less hope of being saved. Less and less of optimistic thinking about going home. As I lay there scared, confused and hungry, my salty, warm tears ran down my face onto my dry lips. I silently pleaded to God to deliver me from this disaster. I prayed harder than I ever prayed in my life pleading, begging God for mercy. After a while, I closed my eyes to sleep, at least that way in my dreams, I could be free from this nightmare.

CHAPTER VII

The Man Of The House

I awakened in peace. A welcoming change from the previous times that I've been here in this hellhole. As I slowly looked around the room, the same funky ass mattresses were still across the walls, and that lonely ass lamp was still standing with a ray of some artificial light. I was distracted by the same depressing ass surroundings and the smell of that funky ass mildew. But only briefly until my eyes caught Max's blood shot eyes staring right at me. I didn't even hear that squeaking wooden door opening or that tray of torment wheels squealing, alarming me of his arrival. He was looking at me in disgust, as if I was an ungrateful mut. Not taking his eyes off me, he sat quietly in the same chair that I was once bound to when this madness began.

Beside him was the same cart that carried his tools of distress. The redolence of fresh hot food was near as the steam flowed through the air into my nostrils, blocking out the awful stench of that mildew. The cart carried food and a clear cup of water or what appeared to be water, along with his tools. He gently rose from the chair and pushed the cart next to the bed. Max pressed the controller button hanging on the side of the bed to sit me upright.

"This is going to be our last chat, Antonio," Max said as if he was worn out.

He took off the shackles that confined my hands and placed the tray of food on my lap. Chicken noodle soup, a bag of plain Lays potato chips, and a bottle of water. I thought for a second, *I could throw the hot soup in his face and bash the metal tray across his head, then beat him until he bled to death.* Reality sunk in, I'm weak, my legs are still in shackles, and he's bigger and stronger than me. I sat there mad as hell because I couldn't do anything, so I ate. Like a homeless derelict that has been without food, I ate.

"I want you to eat and get your strength up and talk, Antonio. Okay? I know you thought you had a *Captain Save-a-Hoe* in here yesterday. Actually, HE could be your hero, or HE could be your demise. It's ALL up to you, Antonio, how this plays out. The ball is in your court. It was my fiancé, the main reason, the only reason you are here. I've already heard his side of this shit repeatedly and it sounded like BULLSHIT each and every time! It doesn't make sense to me, and when shit doesn't make sense to me, that means there's more to the story or it's a lie."

Max proceeded, "As you already know, Antonio, I hate liars! In either case, if he didn't tell me the whole story, it would be deception, and that's still lying! He will be punished accordingly, I promise you! I want to hear your side. People always say, 'There's two sides to a story'. I'm going to tell you my side of the story, the truth. Then you will tell me your side, and maybe we can figure out this shit together."

Max began to tell his truth, "I work a lot as a nurse as I have told you already. I am not just a nurse, I am the Chief Nursing Officer, the CNO. My salary is $370K per year, Antonio. This house was a gift from my parents along with other estates that they owned, as well as $10M in life insurance. I take good care of my business, and I was making sure my fiancé's business was taken care of also. His bills were paid in full every month. I gave him a healthy allowance every week for clothing, food, entertainment, or whatever he wanted to use it for. He drove my Mercedes Benz AMG GT 53 because that is the car he chooses to drive out of all the other ones. My plan was to get him his own car and everything he wanted in his name once we were married. I didn't mind that, in fact, I loved being the provider, HIS provider. I was his, and he was mine as far as I was concerned.

Him being a flight attendant, I knew he had to travel a lot, and I knew he would be away from home a great deal of time. He even bought me a puppy so I wouldn't be lonely when he traveled. That meant the world to me. It made me feel like he really cared and loved me. Whenever, and I mean whenever he came home, he had a hot home cooked meal to eat, a hot bath waiting, clean clothes, and his uniforms were ironed and ready for his next trip. Not to mention I was willing and ready to do whatever to please HIM! I wasn't into sharing him. Call me old-fashioned or selfish, but what was mine, was mine! Sometimes he wanted to have threesomes and I obliged. Other times he wanted four or five dudes to come over at a time, masculine and feminine guys, I went along with that also.

It would often become an all-out orgy. Whatever we did, we did it together! If we wanted to fuck around with anyone, we brought them home or to wherever we were and we did it together! I didn't quite like doing it because I didn't like seeing him with his ass up in the air getting rammed by anyone but me. Even though he was my bottom, I didn't like watching him fuck someone else either! The irony of it is, it turned me on! It just made me feel some type of way. I was jealous to see him enjoying someone else fucking him and making him feel good, but I was invested in watching it. I had to see it, so I drank to loosen up, and it became more palatable to watch.

I couldn't turn away from looking. It was like watching live porn right in my own home: in the living room, bedroom, kitchen, all over the house. I would record him, watch him, and listen to him moan out in ecstasy while being taken to the highest levels of orgasms. When he was away for long periods, I would watch the recordings of him fucking and jack off because I didn't want to cheat on him. He would get fucked from behind on his hands and knees like a dog on the floor, I would get down on my knees in front of him. Pulling his face up to look me into my eyes, I would squeeze his mouth open and spit in it. Then, I'd shove my dick deep into his mouth and make him choke on it.

The deeper I would propel my meaty cock in and out of his salivating mouth, his hot salvia spewed down to my nutts to the crack of my ass, making my cock pulsating stiffer! My attempt to abuse him and his throat was worthless because the more he sweated and gagged while his nose and eyes watered, the more he seemed to love it! He would grab my ass and force feed himself with my meat! He was a little hot slut, but he was MY SLUT! One of the reasons I wanted to punish him so badly is because when we had our threesomes and orgies, he wouldn't let me top him in front of others! Every time he would be fucking one of them and I would get behind him and try to fuck him, he would push me off him, making me feel inadequate.

I didn't like that shit at all! Even when he was topping the other dudes, I would still get envious. I couldn't understand why, and he didn't care. Although I allowed him to top me in front of the guests, I was slightly embarrassed because he was so feminine and so much smaller than me. Therefore, I took out my aggression on the guests and dick punished them! He just wanted to have a good time, and I wanted him to have a good time. I wanted him to be happy, that's why I allowed all that shit in the first place. I just wanted to be a part of it! I wanted to be with him, connected to him! I wanted him to keep it honest and real with me, as I had always kept it honest and real with him.

Everything was copacetic, well at least that's what my naive ass thought! Things changed for the worse and some shit had hit the fan! This one day, this one particular morning, everything in the dark came to light! He was rushing and running late for a flight as usual. It never made sense to me how he could always be running late. The shit was just dumb to me. I've been on the same job since I've graduated high school and throughout college. I have never been late for work or missed a day of work! I got my degree in nursing and got promoted and kept getting promoted.

I handled my business and kept it pushing while moving forward. I had a graveyard shift that night before his flight.

When I got home that morning from work, right away, I started helping him get his things together. Folding his clothes, ironing his uniforms, looking for missing socks, grabbing his underwear out of the dryer, all of that and some. I even gave him a good blow job while we showered before we left for the airport. I sucked him good while I jacked off. I loved jacking off and sucking on his dick because it was so small, I could just gobble the whole thing inside of my mouth without gagging. He nutted so good and all over my face. He always shot a nice load, and this load didn't disappoint. I wanted to bend him over in the shower and fuck him so I could get my nutt too, but I knew we didn't have time for all of that.

It was also because I didn't want the argument again about me fucking him. The shit was just old at that point, and I was tired of the rejection. I just stood up and licked his cum off my lips and we washed each other up. We rushed to the airport without a minute to spare. While parked, I retrieved his bags out of the trunk. He walked up to me, and we said, 'I love you.' We then hugged and kissed. I grabbed his dick and his neck and jokingly told him don't be giving it away. He smiled, kissed me again, and said, 'Never'.

I stopped by Starbucks, got a caramel macchiato, then went back home. While home, I decided to go ahead and get comfortable and book our trip to get married in Jamaca. The fact that we both flew for free because he was a flight attendant, all I had to do was take care of the hotel, excursions, and the rental car. When I was done paying and booking everything, I was ready to get that nutt I wasn't able to get earlier. Entering our walk-in closet to retrieve our homemade porn DVD's, some lube, and a towel, unbeknownst to me, he left his laptop opened sitting on the dresser. I'm not the snooping type of person and I never have been. Why would I have any reason to snoop if we were honest and open with one another?

Reaching to power off his computer and close it, I couldn't help but notice the Adam 4 Adam website open and glaring! 'Why the fuck would he STILL have a gay hook-up account?' I questioned myself. I'm not going to lie, I had an account on there back in the day. Hell, everyone had one. I deleted it when we became a couple, and I thought he deleted his as well! I guess I thought wrong, well shit, I know I'm wrong now! Curiosity overwhelmed me with a slight bit of rage. I skimmed through his profile, and I saw messages back and forward from you two which led me to go check his Facebook messenger because YOU asked him why he was sending you messages on A4A and not on messenger! *What the fuck,* I thought?!

This sneaky little prick! We had access to each other's Facebook, so of course I went to check his direct messages and guess what, Antonio? His messenger displayed catalogs upon catalogs of messages between you both! Pictures, videos, ALL OF IT! Videos that led me to a link to access his OnlyFans page, WHICH I DIDN'T EVEN KNOW HE HAD! THAT sent me down a rabbit hole that I couldn't pull myself out of, Antonio! It was like being glued to watching a train wreck! The more I read and watched, the more hurt I was, but my hurt could not stop me from continuing which brought on more hurt.

I hope you know 'YOU' wasn't the only one, although he claimed to love you just as much as you claimed you love him! You motherfuckers don't know a damn thing about love! Not real love! True, unconditional love! You both make me sick! All you know about is lust and instant gratification!

I've tried and I've tried to give him a good home and some stability! I tried to be there for him, to love him, and hold him whenever he was going through something. That bastard gave me an STD twice, and I stood by his side! Thinking about it, he probably got them from your low life ass! Lay down with dogs and you're bound to get up with fleas! I gave him love and he gave me fucking gonorrhea and then less than a year later syphilis! I had freaking spots breaking out all over my body!

I didn't know what the fuck was going on AND I WORK IN THE MEDICAL FEILD! What the fuck I look like walking around the hospital with dark spots on my face and hands that my scrubs couldn't cover. I had them all over me from the top of my head to literally the bottom of my feet! I researched it and researched it. I didn't have a clue that I had another STD. Not until my co-worker told me it was syphilis! Do you know how embarrassing that was for me, Antonio? How freaking disgusting I felt? Do you, Antonio? Do You KNOW?! Answer me DAMMIT!"

"No, no I, I, I don't know. I didn't know. I'm sorry that happened to you, Max. I, I am really sorry, man."

"You are sorry, Antonio! A sorry piece of shit! I'm tired, Antonio. I'm fed up with the bullshit, his bullshit, your bullshit, ALL OF THE BULLSHIT! You better come correct with the truth or one or BOTH OF YOU are going to get seriously hurt or DIE! One of you is going to suffer for this pain I'm feeling! I don't deserve this! I was faithful and loyal to him! I dedicated my time to him. I gave my heart and energy to HIM! I thought we were truly in love with each other! I thought we were soulmates! You better get your story together, Antonio, and tell me what's going on. Or tell me a lie if you dare! It's your choice, Antonio. But I promise you, if you think I've been hurting you or torturing you, I'm going to make you HATE that you ever met him, and you're going to HATE that I didn't kill you swiftly. I wanted to kill you when I brought you here, but I chose to sample you to see what all the hype was about.

You are a fucking joke AND so is HE for ruining what WE had for a NOTHING ASS BUM LIKE YOU! GOT DAMMIT you motherfuckers are going to realize, I AM THE MAN OF THIS HOUSE! I deserve respect! I deserve to be appreciated! YOU fucking maggots eat my fucking trash! You are trifling maggots! The both of you are trifling maggots that leach on good people like me!"

CHAPTER VIII

Miami Sizzle

"Have you ever been to Miami Sizzle, Antonio?" Max asked, as if he knew something that I didn't know. As if he had something on me, or something over me.

"Yes, Max. I've been to Miami Sizzle. I've been there quite a few times. What are you getting at? I mean, what EXACTLY do you want to know, Max?!"

I knew the clique I ran with at Miami Sizzle or anywhere wouldn't give a nigga like Max a second look. Me and my boys were not the type that would fuck around with the likes of him. The only reason I even entertained Max was because he lured me in with money, and I was being greedy. My friends and I were young twinks, all shades of black, fit, and beautiful. We were fine as hell with great careers. Travelers of the world, free spirits, and we stayed in the finest hotels for free. Trade wanted us! The Latino boys wanted us. The Puerto Rican boys and Dominican boys wanted us. The un-melanated boys couldn't have us and hated us because we all paid them dust, no mind, and no time. None of us wanted any pink meat.

I knew I didn't fuck with it. We were all sickening, and we all knew it. Cis women couldn't stand us either and the feelings were mutual. As much as fish couldn't stand us, it was just as much that they wanted us. Wanting us to slay their hair because they didn't know how to do their own. Wanting us to beat their face because when they did their own make-up, they wound up looking like clowns or looking like they were ready for the casket. Most of their men secretly wanted us and some of us secretly had them. Foolish and stupid. They reminded me of my mama. How the fuck you gone fight me, your own FUCKING SON, over some fuck nigga that I told you kept groping me every time he came over! We only fucked with men on our level. Older or younger, it didn't matter.

The older ones were sugar-daddies, and the younger ones were toys and playthings. If a twink was good looking, had some good ass, good dick or both, that was a plus as far as I was concerned. If an older generous gentleman had a good job with benefits or a pension, that was a plus for me especially if we're not fucking! They became regular clientele. We ACCEPTED those that were worthy. Not tired, old, lame ass mothafucka's like Max!

"I want to know about this year. I want to know EXACTLY ABOUT THIS YEAR, ANTONIO!" Max yelled, bringing my full attention back to his bloodshot eyes. "THIS year in Miami. Wasn't this year at Miami Sizzle special for you? I know that you've been there every year for the last four years with my fiancé since you became a FLIGHT ATTENDANT, a fucking sky waitress!

You don't do shit! A fucking whore is what you are! A whore is what you both are! What you both do is nothing compared to what I do! I digress, didn't this year make your trip to Maimi special, Antonio?

"It was the same old shit," I answered, feeling irritated hearing his same line of questioning about MY business. Who is his fiancé? There are a lot of niggas in my dm's all the fucking time! Who fucked up and left their shit opened for him to find out so much shit about me?! The fact that he knows how many times I've been there is weird. I wasn't even keeping track, the fuck!

"This year, Antonio, this year in particular, who were all with you in Miami? Who did you hang out with? Who did you fuck? Who gave you that ring on your finger?!"

The monster in Max resonated once again as his facial expression went from semi- calm to an angry maniac. I didn't want any more smoke.

"I... I hung out with a few people. I'm pretty sure, no, I, I know your dude wasn't—" Before I could finish, Max interrupted, "My fiancé, he's my fiancé, Antonio!"

"Well, I know your fiancé wasn't there."

"Why are you so sure of that? How do you know that with so much certainty? Who was there with you? Who was all there, Antonio? What happened when you got there DAMMIT?!"

"Okay, okay, relax, man. I'm just saying the dudes that I chilled with are the same ones I've been hanging with for years, not just within the last nine months. I got to Miami the day before Sizzle began. My homie Tyrone picked me up at the airport around 1:30 in the afternoon."

"Who is Tyrone? What does he look like? Where did you meet him? Tell me about him and about your relationship with him."

"Ty and I met at flight attendant school in Memphis four years ago. We were both eighteen and fresh out of high school. He's 6 feet, dark chocolate, about your complexion. He's slim, nice ass, average dick size, except it was thick like a beer can. I loved riding on his dick and grinding on it because it was like one of those thick fat butt plugs. Anyway, he has dark brown eyes and long, black hair past his shoulders.

Anyway, Tyrone already had the rental car and the suite booked at the Hotel AKA Brickwell. We did our usual shit, stopped by Brickwell Station Liquor and got a couple cases of alcohol for the weekend activities. We ate at Paperfish restaurant and had a few cocktails. After the restaurant, we went to the hotel to hang out, smoke, and drink until everyone else got in that evening."

"So, you two just hung out in the hotel room and drank?" Max asked in disbelief.

"Yeah, we unpacked, showered, kicked it for a while — smoked and drank."

"So, Antonio, you're telling me, you two little pricks didn't do anything but CHILL OUT?!"

"Mane, what the FUCK do you want to know?!" I asked, frustrated.

"Okay, Antonio, okay. You want to play games. We can play," Max said, quickly standing up and walked away from the bed with the cart in tow.

He swiftly walked towards the door.

"No, no wait!" I yelled, not knowing what the hell he meant or what he was going to do. "He sucked my dick! Tyrone sucked my dick! Before we could even make it inside of the hotel room, he sucked my dick right there at the room front door. I repeatedly put the room key card into the door slide, and it wouldn't open. Tyrone called the front desk and the hotel receptionist said she would send someone up with a new key card and it would be a few minutes."

Antonio began to describe what happened Tyrone said and did next, "I see that you're freeballing today, Tony." Tyrone said, rubbing on my gentiles. "Your print has been calling my mouth since I picked you up from the airport. That thang is thanging, swanging, and hanging." Licking his lips, he went on, "Well, since we have to wait . . ." He pulled my joggers down to my knees, "let me shallow you up first before these bitches get here and hog you up." Dropping down before me, Ty put my dick in his mouth and performed fellatio."

Max's inquisitiveness got the best of him, because he left the cart by the door and came and sat back down in the chair beside me.

"Go on, Antonio," Max requested.

I nervously continued, "Tyrone grabbed my limp dick and put it in his mouth until it was down his throat. Grabbing my balls, he squeezed and massaged them. Constantly spitting on my dick and balls while teasing the head with his tongue, he got me rock hard and ready for action. I wrapped his long silky jet-black hair around my hand and palmed the back of his head with my other hand. Force feeding him my cum shooter to the back of his throat in and out his sultry, wet mouth was for his rapture and mine. Hence, I plunged my dick deeper and deeper past his tonsils, attempting to make him heave because I knew he loved that shit; he was just as nasty as me. Ty put both of my balls in his mouth and slurped on them while jacking off my solid-hard dick firmly and rapidly.

'Ooooooh, shit, Ty!' I yelled. I was about to nutt. I was… until I heard the elevator doors open and voices. 'Ty, get up! Get up, Tyrone!' I had to grab him because he wouldn't stop! I pulled him up by his shirt while trying to pull my joggers up at the same time. I knew someone had to see it. Out of the seven people that exited the elevator, at least one of them got a glimpse, I'm sure of it. I know the porter seen us because his fat, goofy looking ass had a stupid grin on his face as he approached us.

Opening the door for us, he handed us a new key card and walked away. Ty was such a freak; he didn't care who saw what. He would have finished me off right there in front of those people if I had let him. As soon as the door was closed, Ty locked it and ripped off all his clothes. He ran right pass me and the hot tub and jumped his lil ebony self butt naked ass on the bed. On his hands and knees, he gestured with his finger for me to come to him. 'Damn, Ty, you don't want to wait until tonight when everyone gets here?' I asked with a devilish smirk on my face. Knowing I didn't want to wait either, I strolled over to him. Ty gave me some of the best sloppy toppy I've ever had. He knew I loved getting head from him."

"Did he give you a blow job?"

"Yeah, he did, Max."

"Was it good? Did you fuck him, or did he fuck you?"

"We fucked each other, man, damn!"

"How many more people were coming, Antonio?"

I didn't understand why Max wanted to know about such intimate details of my life. I told him I didn't know his fiancé too many times. I could never see myself even chilling with anyone that would be attached to his insecure ass. Who would ever or could ever be his friend, let alone be his fiancé. I went along with his line of questioning out of fear of what would happen if I didn't.

"Three, three more," I answered, hoping I could just finish the story.

"Who were they? What do they look like? Where are they from? Were you sexually active with any of them?" asked Max.

"Robbie, Jacob, and . . . and Rodney from Saint Martin. I already told you about Tyrone."

"So, where did you meet the others?"

"Different places. Robbie is a flight attendant that I met on Adam 4 Adam. He's the one that inspired and convinced me to go to flight attendant school and quit stripping."

"Tell me about Robbie."

"Like I said, I met Robbie on A4A back in 2018. He's cute, about 5'1", a little lighter than you, low haircut, very small build, and a small dick. We had a meet and fuck at my crib and became Friends With Benefits (FWB). I really enjoyed his company because I was sadly in a dark place in my life at the time. Robbie would come over, and we would talk, play cards, drink, smoke, watch movies, and fuck. He would let me fuck him every now and again but mainly he would fuck me. Taking my dick was too much for him. I didn't mind because he fucked me good even though I'm a size queen, and besides, I liked the way he fucked me and treated me. He really was sweet and into me and wanted me to himself. Unfortunately, I was still in my hoe phase so he would do stupid shit like bang on my door and hop over my balcony when I would have other niggas over.

"What about Jacob?"

"He's a flight attendant also. Robbie introduced me to him a few years ago when he and I flew to New York in the beginning of 2020 to visit him. Harlem was Jacob's hometown. He was a straight New Yorker with the whole package, accent, swagger and all, it turned me on. Jacob is about 5'9", caramel complexion, slim, short cut afro, full big smokers' lips, and carried about a good 9-inches of meat between his legs. The first night that we chilled at Jacob's place, we drank, smoked some weed, and had a threesome. Shit got funny because while I was riding Jacob's dick, Robbie got jealous and pushed me off Jacob. I guess he was mad because I was enjoying myself a little too much.

Jacob got some good dick, and I loved that he would put it deep inside my hole. He fucked me good. It was hilarious to me that Robbie got upset and pushed me off Jacob, but not at all to Robbie. I really didn't give a fuck about it too much, and I think my nonchalant attitude pissed Robbie off even more. The next evening, Jacob took us to an underwear party in his neighborhood just up the street from 139th where he lived."

"What the hell is an underwear party!?" Max asked with confusion.

"It's a party that is EXACTLY what it sounds like, Max."

"Well, explain it to me, Antonio, because I've never heard of such a party. You can cut the condescending ass attitude out of your fucking voice also, Antonio!"

"An underwear party is a party where men get together at a designated place, walk around with nothing but their underwear on, mingle, drink, dance, and fuck if they want to. Jacob, Robbie, and I had to walk to a specific bodega, stand in front of it while Jacob texted a special number. Once we all were seen through binoculars from the location and approved of, Jacob was given the address and apartment number where the party was being held. We walked to the address and entered the building. Trade was outside and inside everywhere. We got on the elevator and rode up to the 34th floor. We knocked on door #333 and paid a $10 entrance fee.

We were given a ticket and an empty box. We were to go into the bathroom one at a time and put all our clothing, except our underwear and socks, into the box along with our phones. Jacob went into the bathroom first and came out with his plaid boxers and socks on. He handed security his box and placed his ticket in his sock. Robbie and I debated on who would go in next. I made him go in before me. Robbie came out of the bathroom wearing purple laced see through assless lingerie with thigh high purple fish net stockings with his little sexy ass."

"And you?" Max asked.

"I went into the bathroom, took a perk, a swig out of my flask, got undressed, and sprayed some perfume on. Once I packed my things inside of the box, I looked in the mirror to make sure that I was straight. I came out of the bathroom wearing my pink Pink Panther crop top, my pink jock strap for easy access, and my knee-high pink furry boots. I placed my box ticket inside of my boots and handed the box to the security guy. Security escorted the three of us into the living room where there were guys sitting on the sofa talking. Some guys were dancing, and some guys were in the kitchen drinking.

There was a bartender selling different alcoholic beverages and snacks. Security then showed us the two rooms where we could enter and do whatever we desired for the evening. The first room was a dark private room broken off into a section of four, for one-on-one sessions. The second room was dimly lit with green LED lights and had about four mattresses on the floor. It was filled with guys everywhere. Tall, short, well built, slim, skinny, but all fine. Some were standing talking, some were on the mattresses fucking, and some were on their knees sucking dick. A few tables throughout the room had bowls of condoms, mini lubes, and bath towels.

"Jacob said, 'This is the room I always go in. You girls do you, I'm gonna do me.' I was definitely ready for some action," Antonio told Max. "I was feeling extra sexy with all my pink on, and I already knew that my jock strap had my ass sitting upright and tight. I watched Jacob grab a random fem boy by the hand and they disappeared to the other side of the room. Some caramel skin body builder type guy whispered something in Robbie's ear, and Robbie shook his head in acceptance, and the guy picked him up. Robbie's arms were around his neck, and his legs were around the guy's waist. They went off, but not out of my eyesight. I looked around the room to see what I wanted to get into. Questioning myself if I wanted to get fucked or fuck, I answered myself, why not both.

My eyes zeroed in on this fine, smooth, blacker than midnight man standing and conversing with three other men off to the side of the room. He was about 5'10", 165 pounds, athletic build, six-pack, small waist, stacked cakes, with long locs with gold tips at the ends flowing down his back. He had couple of earrings in each ear, a septum piercing, a nipple piercing, tattoos all over his body, and was wearing a white and blue Calvin Klein jock strap. I approached him, made eye contact, and without saying anything, I pulled his jock strap down to his feet and fell to my knees before him. I took hold of his limp uncut meat, pulled his foreskin back, and placed his chocolate Hersheys bar inside of my mouth. His not saying a word was absolutely my green light.

As his dick began to get hard it formed into an upward curve. I thought to myself, *DAMN!* Placing my hands on the floor before me, I leaned in on him, and I continued sucking his dick, and he began to fuck my face. Never have I been fucked by a nigga with a dick with a curve, and I wasn't about to pass up a new adventure to find out what it was giving. I sucked on him with all mouth and no hands, allowing him to freely mouth fuck me until he was on the verge of cumming.

A few minutes in, he grabbed my hair with both hands and started forcing himself in deeper. That let me know that he wanted to cum, so I stopped and got up. I took him by his hand, got a condom, a small bottle of lube, a towel, and led him to an empty spot on one of the mattresses. I placed the bath towel on the mattress and assumed the position, face down and ass up because that's the way I like to get fuck. He put the condom on, massaged lube on his covered dick, and massaged some around, on, and inside of my asshole."

Antonio continued, 'Here you go,' he said, handing me the bottle of lube.

'Thank you, sexy,' I responded, placing the lube in front of me in case I wanted to jack off while he was beating it from the back. *SMACK! SMACK! SMACK!* 'Ooooo, SHIT, papi!,' I said as I turned back to look at him. This nigga smacked my ass cheeks, and I liked it. 'Oh, you like that, lil mama?' He asked. 'Hell, yeah, papi! That shit is hot as fuck! Spank me again, papi.' *SMACK! SMACK! SMACK! SMACK!* That nigga was taking turns smacking the shit out of my ass cheeks and that shit was turning me the fuck on! I never knew I would like something like that but the more he smacked my ass, the more it jiggled and the more it jiggled, the more it excited me."

Next, Antonio began to reiterate how the evening proceeded. "Ooooo, yeah, papi, SMACK that fat ass and slide that sexy ass crooked dick up in me!"

"You got it, lil mama," he said as he delivered just what I ordered. Holding my cheeks wide open . . . "DAMN, boy, your hole is pretty and pink as fuck! Just looking at it makes my dick throb."

He slowly inserted his penis into my lubricated anus. Once fully inserted, I felt his curved dick bump my prostate. I knew it was about to go down! The propulsion of his velocity gradually accelerated to the rhythm of me backing up and moving forward with his rhythm. Soon, the harder he pounded me the harder I backed my ass up to get him in deeper. It didn't take us long to find our groove as we began to moan together with pleasure. His curved dick started pounding my prostate and my moans became louder than his. Getting cocky and rightfully so, he set in motion to thrash my tight hole as it squeezed on his dick causing slippery, and very warm friction between us. While he was smacking my ass with one hand and pulling my hair with the other, I arched my back more as I lay my chest completely on the towel allowing my ass to sit up perfectly for him to dig in deeper.

"AAAAAHHH SHIT, lil mama, I'm bout to bust this nutt!" he said, gripping the back of my jock strap, as his thrust became rapid.

"OOOOO! YAASSS, GET IT, PAPI, GET IT! YAAASSS, BABY, FUCK THIS ASS!"

He was fucking me so damn GOOD and HARD! I forgot about lubing up and jacking off while he was fucking me. I just went with it.

"SMACK MY ASS, PAPI! SMACK MY ASS!

SMACK! SMACK! SMACK! SMACK! SMACK! SMACK!

"YAAAASSSS, PAPI, FUCK THIS PUSSY! BEAT THAT SHIT UP! BEAT IT UP PAPI!"

"OOOOOO! NIGGAAAA, OOOOOO! SHIIIIII I'M BUUUUSSTIIIIING!!"

He quickly pulled out of my hole and pulled the condom off his dick to beat his nutt out. I turned around expeditiously facing him on my knees and grabbed hold of his dick and jacked him off. His nutt shot all over my face and shirt as he groaned, moaned, and trembled. I leaned down still holding on to his still hard curved dick and sucked out the remaining drops.

"OOOOOO, BAAABY, OOOOOO DAAAMN! OOOOOO, AAAaaahhhh!" he moaned as I finished him off.

"Did you like that papi?" I asked, already knowing the answer.

"HELL to the YES! That shit was fire, lil mama, DAMN! I haven't busted like that in a long time. Your ass was just bouncing and taking all my dick. My shit still hard as fuck! Look at it."

"Yeah, I see it papi," I said, holding his Hershey bar in my hand. "I would do a round two with you, but I see a lil dude over there that I want to do what you just did to me."

"DAMN, lil mama, you top too?"

"I do it all, papi. I'm a girl with many talents."

"Well, shit I'm verse, so what's good?"

"Oooohhhh, shit, you want to try my princess?" I asked, pulling my dick out of my jock strap.

"DAMN, nigga even your dick is fucking pretty! You're a pretty ass mothafucka!"

"That's why they call me Pretty Red, papi," I said as I grabbed the back of his head and guided his mouth towards my princess for some much-needed head.

"And Rodney?" Max interjecting, disrupting Antonio's account of that night.

"Rodney came in the picture when Robbie, Jacob, and I were on the way to Saint Martin for a quick last-minute vacation in 2020. We met him working on our flight and he invited us to his beach house. Robbie canceled our hotel reservations at the Morgan Resort Spa & Village, and we stayed at Rodney's place for the week instead. Rodney showed us the time of our lives being that he is a native of the island. We didn't want for anything. Food, drinks, alcohol, weed, coke, male strippers and escorts, Rodney took care of it all. He even had some of the locals come party with us."

"What does Rodney look like, Antonio? Did you guys fuck?"

"He's 5 feet, dark skin, locs, skinny, and had the biggest dick out of all of us. It's always those skinny niggas packing the most meat. He is at least 11-inches long, uncut, and he's a full bottom. I used to want him to fuck me so bad, but he would only let me fuck him or we just sucked each other off or both. He could take some dick so that was a plus. Jacob, Ty, Robbie, and I would run a train on Rodney. I used to beat the breaks off his lil petite ass. The thing that made me not fuck with Rodney too tight is the fact that he is a serious weed head. He would smoke the first thing in the morning and all throughout the day. We all hooked up maybe five or six times out of the year, depending on our schedules. L. A. Pride, New York Pride, Memphis Pride, Maimi Sizzle, Atlanta for Labor Day weekend, Saint Martin, and a couple of cruises."

"You all would all get together and have fuck parties, is that it, Antonio?" Max asked, crossing his arms and sitting back in the chair. "I mean, well, you all travel all over the place, drink, smoke, fuck each other, and fuck other people. At the end of the day, it is an all-out fuck feast though, am I right?!"

"If that's what you want to call it, then I guess so, Max."

"No, Antonio, what would you call it? It sounds to me that all of you are a bunch of hoes! What would you call it?! You all got together and partied, drink, smoked, fucked, and had orgies!"

"We are all single gay grown ass men that enjoyed each other's company, that's what the FUCK I would call it!"

"HOLD UP, PARTNER!! First of all, one of them isn't SINGLE, he is engaged, spoken for, and STILL IS! And another of your so-called girls is actually married! Married to a woman that he has children with! Repulsive, nauseating, DL lying whores! That's what all of you are!"

"None of my friends are engaged, and none of them had a ring on that indicated such! I know none of them are married to fish and have kids with fish! You got us fucked up with somebody else. I don't know your dude and that's on that!"

"That night who fucked who?! I'm really curious to know how that all worked out. Antonio, where did you get that ring from?" Max asked, as he if he didn't hear or care about a thing I had just said and knew more than I did about what I was talking about.

"I don't know, I've had it for a while now."

"Oooh, so you've had it for a while, really? Sooooo, did you buy it? Did you find it? Did someone give it to you?!"

"MAX, I guess I bought it, I don't fucking remember!"

"May I see it?" Max asked.

"I can't get it off! My finger has been swollen since I've been here if you haven't fucking noticed!"

Max looked at me as if he didn't believe me.

"I can't get it off, seriously! My fucking finger is swollen! Probably from laying in this fucking bed for so long! If you wanted it, why didn't you take it when you took my watch and my other shit!"

"Oh, okay, Antonio, okay," Max said, as he stood up and walked towards the door. "I'll be back." Nodding his head, he pushed the cart out of the room. The door squeaked open and closed as he shut it behind him.

Shacking my head, I thought to myself, *this is some straight bullshit!* I hope he wasn't lying when he said this is our last talk. I'm so sick and tired of this, I don't know how much more of this I can take! I can't take it anymore! Lord, please forgive me. Please make this end. I know it's said, *you won't put more on me than I can bare. I can't bare anymore of this, Lord, I just can't! I won't!*

CHAPTER IX

A Ring Of Truth

Max can have this fucking ring if that's what it takes for him to release me. I looked at it and tried again to remove it from my swollen finger; all in vain. I just don't understand why he didn't take it off my finger when he stole my other jewelry if it was so damn important. What's the deal with this fucking ring. I've had it for at least two years. Okay, think, *where did I buy it . . . shit, I don't remember.* I bought a lot of jewelry, and I've been given a lot of jewelry. Who remembers shit like that? After laying there and thinking for a while, the door opened.

Pushing in the cart first with the same silver tray on top with his tools of torment. Again, Max was dressed in his scrubs with his purple latex gloves on. This time he was also wearing a KN95 mask and medical safety goggles. *This can't be good, this ain't right.* Anxiety and panic started to set in. My heart started to race; my forehead and hands began to sweat. I felt nauseous suddenly.

"Please, please, Max, whatever you're thinking about doing, please don't do it! PLEEEAAASSSEE DON'T DO IT!", I cried, begged, and shouted. I sat up as much as I could while still being shackled to the bed. Tears instantly started flowing down my face. "Please, have mercy, I'm sorry, I'm so sorry!" I cried.

"I know you're SORRY, Antonio, I know that already! You're a sorry prick! You are a sorry human being! You are a sorry waste of space! BOTH OF YOU FUCKERS ARE SORRY, PATHETIC, LOW LIFE SCUM! Your mothers should have pulled you both out of their pussies with wire coat hangers and flushed you both down the toilet! Everybody plays the fool! I'm just a fucking fool! I try to be there for people, my love ones, MY SO-CALLED LOVER, MY SO-CALLED SOULMATE, MY FUCKING PARTNER, MY FIANCÉ! You GIVE your HEART, your SOUL, your ENERGY, and your MIND! YOU BOTH played a fool out of me!"

Jumping into the conversation, "I'm a fool too, Max! I don't even know what's going on here! I'm— "

"HA, HA, HA, HA, HA!" Max laughed, harder and harder as if he was completely insane.

Max pushed my chest, and I fell back onto the bed. I was too scared to try and fight him again, because I knew it would make things worse. I laid there trying to be good, trying not to cause any more problems. Max grabbed my right hand and chained it down closer to the bed. He pushed the cart to the other side of the bed. At this point, I was shaking uncontrollably, my sweat mixed with my tears, and they flowed together down my face.

"I, I got to go to the bathroom, Max! I have to go shit! PLEASE, PLEASE, I have to go really bad, Max!"

Ignoring my plea, my begging, and my tears, Max grabbed my left wrist with his left hand and applied so much pressure, I couldn't feel my blood flowing into my hand. With the same hand he spread my fingers apart. With his right hand, he reached towards the silver tray and grabbed the pair of surgical scissors.

"NOOOO! NOOOOO!" I screamed to the heavens above.

Max pulled my ring finger and under the ring . . . *SNIP! CRUNCH!* . . . is all I heard. What I saw was my blood gushing from a hole between my pinky and middle finger, splattering across his mask and goggles, then onto my face and chest. I saw my finger with that cheap ass ring attached to it fall onto my chest and roll down to my lap, leaving a bloody trail. I couldn't lift my head up. I just looked at my finger laying there motionless as tears and blood blurred my vision and rolled down my cheeks. Snot poured from my nose. I couldn't move, I couldn't speak, I couldn't do anything but stare. I was in total shock. I just sat there and relieved myself. All my energy was depleted; my fight was gone. My faith was gone.

I had no strength, no words, and no prayers left in me. I felt Max tilt my head to the side and inject something into me, most likely more of the same shit. At that point, I didn't care. I didn't give a shit anymore. I just wanted to die and for this to finally be over with once and for all. I slumped over and droll began leaking from my mouth. Not really feeling too much pain, I assumed that it was either because I was in shock or because of whatever he injected in me. What have I done to this man to deserve this? Who is his fucking fiancé? So many questions, and I didn't have any answers. I just didn't understand. I didn't get it.

CHAPTER X

Tainted Love

"Tony . . . Tony, Anthony!"

What voice I heard I did not know, but I did know it wasn't Max's voice. It was a soft-spoken gentle voice. I wasn't sure if it was a woman's voice, but it sounded familiar. A voice of comfort and security, but I couldn't place it. *Maybe I am dreaming.* It was all a dream, that's all it could have been. I hoped and prayed I wasn't dreaming and that it was actually someone there to save me. Please wake me up and take me out of this nightmare. I felt a warm and tender hand rubbing my face. I couldn't open my eyes. It was as if I was having a lucid dream in a nightmare that I couldn't wake up from. I could hear the voice, and I was certain it wasn't the voice of that fucking monster. The one who had stolen me away from my life. The one that stole me away from everything and everyone I loved.

The painful throbbing in my left hand from that unauthorized amputation was starting up again. My anxiety began to rise, which made me realize it wasn't a dream at all, but a sad and horrifying reality. Such pain could never be a part of a dream. The heat of someone's hand was still caressing my face. I could smell the familiar scent of perfume that this mystery person was wearing. I just couldn't put it together; my mind was too far gone. I couldn't place it or concentrate. What's going on? What is this? This was playing with my emotions, and the little bit of sanity I had left.

"WHAT IS THIS?!" I screamed out with my eyes still glued shut from dried tears and dried blood. I wanted to see who was talking to me and rubbing my face. I attempted to open my eyes again by reaching to rub the crust from them.

"Tony, please wake up, open your eyes. Baby, I'm so sorry, I'm sorry. I had no idea Max would do something like this. Please open your eyes, Antonio, please. It's me, it's Robbie."

ROBBIE, IT'S ROBBIE! That's what I heard. He said Robbie. What the fuck? I shook my head vigorously and again struggled to rub my eyes open. Finally, they cracked open — blurry, but open. True enough, when I was able to focus, it was indeed Robbie. He was leaning over me and rubbing my face, caressing the newly grown-in beard on my chin. I didn't even know or realize I had grown a beard until I felt his fingers flowing through it and stroking my chin. Just soothing me and comforting me like he always did.

I remembered how good it used to feel lying next to Robbie in bed while he would caress me until I fell asleep. His softness, his body odor, the way his body fit perfectly against me. We laid together naked and free, grown men intertwining our souls beyond classifications of gender. Laying together in brief moments in time, I felt the contentedness of pleasure, passion, and peace.

Those lovely memories quickly came to a halt once the actuality of the situation that I was in set in. The truth is I realized where I was. Robbie was here with me, but why? He was dressed to impress as always, but he looked different. He didn't look like the Robbie that I knew. He looked overly stressed, exhausted, and lost, in such a way I had never seen him. I was in fucked up shape myself but seeing Robbie looking so helpless made me hurt even more.

"Wha... what the fuck, Robbie?! What's going on?! Why are you here?! Do you know this monster?! Do you know this man, Robbie?! That BEAST?! Are yo... you, you the one he's engaged to?! How long have you known that I was here?! How come you didn't call the police?! Are you in on this shit, Robbie?! Are you— "

Before I could ask any more questions, Robbie sighed with tears streaming down his face. "NO, NO, Antonio, I would never have been a part of this. I would never do anything to hurt you, Tony! You know I love you. I love you so much, Antonio. I never loved Max. That black bastard! I begged Max not to do this! He promised me he would leave you out of our mess. I told him we were going to work it out. I told him I was going to leave you alone. I swore that I would! I made it clear to him that you didn't want me like that, and I wanted to be with someone that wanted me! Someone that loved me."

He proceeded, "I assured Max he was the only one for ME! He promised me that you weren't an issue anymore. You must believe me, Antonio! I'm going to call the police and the paramedics right now. You're going to be alright, and they're going to get you out of here. Everything is going to be okay, Tony, I promise. Everything is going to be just fine! I love you! I love you, baby, you—"

"Robbie, why do you keep telling me how much you love me? What do you mean you love me?! Love me how, Robbie? We're boys, homie, lovers, friends, Friends With Benefits! We fucked around but we ALL fucked around. WE ALL had an understanding that it wouldn't get serious like that between any of us! There was a pact we all made — no serious feelings, no strings. I was cool with that, you were cool with that, we all were cool with that! What the fuck, Robbie?!"

"You told me you loved me, Tony. You made me believe that we had a chance, and that we could have grown from there! I was convinced that you would grow to love me as much as I love you."

"NO, NO, Robbie, you ain't getting it! I loved your company and spending time with you. Seeing you smile and being happy made me happy. I loved you for being your authentic self. Talking to you to get shit off my chest and vice versa was cool and all. You listened to me, and you were there for me, I loved that. I put everything up front with you from the beginning! You lied to me! Out of all people, Robbie, YOU lied to me! I didn't know you were engaged, the fuck! None of us knew you were engaged!

Out of all people, you could have told me. I figured you were feeling me, but I didn't know it was this way or this serious! How could the relationships we all had not be enough for you? Now look at me! Look at my fucking hand! That maniac cut off my finger for a fucking ring, a fucking ring that I don't even remember how I got! He cut off my finger, my fucking finger, Robbie!" I repeated that over and over as I looked down at the bloody beige bandages wrapped around my hand.

"Look at my face, Robbie, do you see what he has done to my face with a fucking fly swatter! All my beautiful HAIR IS GONE because Max cut it off with scissors! My teeth were snatched out with pliers, FUCKING WIRE PLIERS because of YOU, ROBBIE! ALL OF THIS SHIT HE'S DONE TO ME IS BECAUSE OF YOU, ROBBIE!" I began to cry and sob like a child. I cried as the rain poured down outside. The harder I cried, the harder it seemed to have rained and thundered.

"Baby, I know. I know you didn't know anything about the ring. You don't deserve any of this! This is my fault! It was me! This is all my fault, Antonio. I am truly sorry. Please forgive me, Antonio, please, I beg of you."

"How? Why? WHY IS THIS YOUR FAULT?! WHY AM I FUCKING HERE, ROBBIE, WHHHHYYYY?!" I yelled.

"It all happened when we were all at Miami Sizzle. Everyone else was high and drunk and fell asleep in the living room that Sunday morning after partying all night. Remember you went into your room, and we stayed up talking and drinking even more. Reminiscing about the good old times how we first met. When you first met me, you assumed I was some little conceited bougie butch queen from the hood. You told me I was too feminine for you to let me hit. I gathered that you were some country bumpkin with pretty privilege who thought his shit didn't stink. We argued and debated for hours and wound-up having sex that night, all night to the break of dawn.

It was a wonderful meet and greet even though it started off as a late-night booty call off Adam 4 Adam. We became friends and our friendship grew into something special, something meaningful. That night in Maimi, I wanted so desperately to tell you about Max and me, and how depressed I was. I didn't want to ruin the night by bringing you down about my problems. Instead, I cried, you held me, and wiped my tears away. You told me that you loved me, and that whatever it was that I was going through, you would love me regardless."

"Robbie! I told you I—"

"I know what you told me, Antonio. I know you didn't mean you loved me the way I wanted you to mean it, but any love coming from you was enough for me. At least it was a start as far as I was concerned. Wiping my tears as they began to flow even more, you kissed them and kissed me. That made me feel sooo special, so loved, and wanted. You grabbed me and embraced me so tightly under you, I felt as if I was floating into your soul without anything to hold on to. Whatever you wanted from me mentally, physically, or spiritually, I was yours. I was YOURS for the taking at that very moment. YOURS for the making of whatever art you wanted to create, at that space in time. I felt and believed I was YOURS! Yours only, I wanted to be.

Instead of fucking me that night like you normally do, for the first time, I felt you made love to me, and I silently cried as I tightly held on to you. You were so gentle and loving. Antonio, you knew exactly how to make me feel. No man has ever made me feel the way you made me feel. When you fuck me or make love to me, I don't even care if I cum or not because it's just that satisfying to me. You laying me on my stomach and slowly deep stroking me, holding me, kissing me on my neck and back was the purest of your love pouring out into me. At least that's what I felt, that's how I feel! It was just you and me, no one was in our world, not even Max. You told me that you loved me and kissed my tears as you made love to me. I wasn't crying because you were hurting me, I was crying because I didn't want you making love to me to ever end but I knew that it would. Eventually we would have to—"

"Yeah, okay," I responded interrupting.

"You told me that you were serious, and I believed you, Tony. When you fell asleep, I took my engagement ring that Max had given me out of my bag and put it on your finger. I wanted you to have it as a token of my love for our love. I knew you wouldn't have known where it came from because you bought so many clothes and so much jewelry when we were all out shopping the day before. Only I knew where it came from and that was fine with me. I told Max that I lost the ring. He told me that it was okay, not to worry about it, and he would get me another one. Some simple crap as always with him. It is a $11,000 ring and he brushed it off like it wasn't a big deal. He didn't even ask me where I think I lost it. All Max wanted to do was buy me and put me on a pedestal in a glass jar so no one would have access to me but him!

After I put the ring on your finger, I kissed your lips and took pictures of us. I posted them on my 'X' account and Instagram under the caption, *'My man is dreaming of me and I'm right here under him.'* I lay beside you and fell asleep under your arms. I've been in love with you since day one, Tony. All these years I have loved you in secret because I know how much you enjoy your freedom. Max and I were together, therefore, there wasn't much else I could pursue with you. I had been with Max for so long, I was comfortable with him, no longer in love with him, just comfortable with him. That's why when Max asked me to marry him, I said yes. I knew that you and I would never have a real chance together. I didn't want to be lonely anymore. Waiting to see you three or four times out of the year and then having to share you with Rodney, Jacob, and Ty was driving me crazy!

I love the other guy's also, Antonio, but what you and I have or had, I felt it was on another level. You and I have a bond, a special bond outside the other guys. I wanted someone full-time, and someone that wanted to be with me full-time! When I'm around you, I can be fem, masculine, a top or bottom, or whatever I want to be! Tony, you accepting me fully and unconfined was the ultimate turn on for me, and it made me love you even more. You explored every part of me and ravished me completely! I could never do that with Max because he made me feel restricted.

Whenever I would try to be myself in public, around his friends or family, he would stare the fear of death into me. Max would lose his mind and scold me like I was his child as soon as we were alone. Wearing the sexy things that I wear around you guys was out of the question as far as Max was concerned. I felt as if I was constantly under a microscope and walking on eggshells around him. That's why I stopped letting him fuck me. It is why I made him come out to his homophobic ass friends and family! When I fuck him, I fuck him out of hate to punish him and embarrass him for the way he made and makes me feel. Denying him the pleasure of penetrating me because he denies me the pleasure of being my true self is my revenge.

Whenever we would have our little sexcapades, I would heavily flirt with the guys we would have over. I would allow them to have sex with me anyway they wanted to while Max sat there getting drunk and recording it all. He was so desperate to keep me, he allowed me to do whatever I wanted to do as long as I did it with him. This is why I made him have threesomes and orgies. Max would have even accepted a threesome with you involved, but I didn't want to share you with him. Honestly, I didn't want to share you with Rodney, Jacob, or Ty. How would I have been able to explain to you who Max truthfully was to me after all these years. My ego wouldn't allow the embarrassment of you or the guys judging me for being with somebody like Max. My love for you outgrew my love for Max or anyone else. I waited to be with you because of the way we communicated and connected without saying a word.

I waited for you because of how you would make me feel sexually, and because the way you gave me permission to sexually satisfy you anyway I wanted to. Max was a virgin when he met me. He was on the Down Low and lusting after young twinks such as I on adult apps when he ran across my profile. Everything he knows about sex, I taught him. You and I know that I was far from a virgin when we met.

We talked about how Wallace got me when I was only eight years old. Although he was twelve, he knew what he was doing, and I definitely didn't. I didn't stop him either, that's why I never said he molested me. Who and how was I going to tell anybody about it. My mom was constantly being beaten by her live-in boyfriend, and it was always a chaotic mad house in our home.

They were both alcoholics and weed heads. My mother was depressed 80% of the time, high and out of it the other 20% of the time. Her boyfriend was out and about cheating and gambling away everything my mom worked for when he wasn't beating the crap out of her. Who could I have told? I had no one to tell, and it didn't feel like I had the need to tell anyone. Wallace introduced me to something that I didn't know I liked. He gave me attention, something that I was lacking at home. Although I was only eight years old, he made me feel wanted and desired. I don't know why I liked what he was doing to me and how he was making me feel but I did. It may be a sad story to some people, but a lot of older boys were touching on me and doing things with me. Hell, I was taught how to give head when I was nine or ten years old by an older boy.

Inevitably, I graduated from boys to men when I became a teenager. Out of all people, Antonio, I know you understand. Max couldn't understand. He would act like he understood, but I knew he really didn't. If he did, he wouldn't treat me the way that he does, or down talk me the way that he does. Max didn't take advantage of me; instead I took advantage of him. He may be book smart, but he is not street smart. Deep down inside, I needed someone on my level, on my playing field. Tony, I only wanted to mess around with you.

You are on my level. We come from the same ghettos and have been through a lot of similar things. Even though I do enjoy having sex with Tyrone, Rodney, and Jacob, they do not compare to you. Jacob is always too demanding and rough. He's not the way that you are, rough and sweet. You get me where you are trying to take me every time our bodies mesh. Ty just wants to give and get head all the time and that gets boring to me.

Don't get me wrong, I love a good dick sucker, and I love sucking some dick, but I wanted more from him. I wanted to beat his hole and for him to beat mine sometimes. I always fantasized about banging him doggie style and pulling on his beautiful hair while beating his hole in. I even fantasized about him banging me missionary with his hair just flying everywhere as he beat the life out of me. His dick was so fat and thick, I couldn't help but wonder how it would have felt inside of me. I just know his booty hole was extra tight because he never gets penetrated.

Rodney on the other hand is strictly bottom, and I couldn't help but wonder what he could do with that 11-inch dildo he was carrying around. Now don't get me wrong, I do love sucking on Rodney's long dick and gaging on it while jacking off. That gets me hot and going. You, Antonio, now you are the whole package, and I love that about you! Good booty, good dick, good head, and a good head giver."

CHAPTER XI

The Beast

"Cut the shit, Robbie, where is Max? How did you get in here past him? I'm curious to know how you finally realized I was fucking here! Weren't you here the other day? Max said you were here. If you were here, I know you heard me screaming and yelling for help! Why didn't you call the police then?"

Robbie gently took hold of my bandaged hand and held on to it as he sat in the chair next to me. "Tony, no, no, I wasn't here! Max lied to you."

"There was somebody in here, Robbie! I heard him arguing with someone! So, who the fuck was it if it wasn't you, Robbie?!"

"I don't know, Tony. I honest to God do not know. I wouldn't lie to you. You have got to believe me!"

"Who the fuck am I supposed to believe, Robbie? What kind of shit do y'all have going on?!"

"Please don't be like that, Tony. There's no telling who he had in here. I am really sorry that this happened to you. Max threatened me that if I didn't stop being with you guys, especially you, that he would hurt you. That's why I promised him that I would stop. As much as I hated it, I had to break it off with you guys because I knew that Max could be dangerous. His temper sometimes becomes unhinged."

"Yeah, ya think, Robbie, the fuck!"

"Yes, Tony, I know, but he's never ever done anything this crazy. He had his suspicions about our guy trips, but I always smoothed things over with him and regained his trust. Me leaving my computer open was a crucial mistake on my behalf. I really messed up. The pictures and videos of all of us having sex was one thing. Max seeing the pictures and videos of us in Miami with you wearing my engagement ring was the final straw as far as he was concerned. He couldn't take seeing you and I boo'd up taking pictures and you making love to me wearing that ring.

Max said it was the ultimate slap in his face, and if I didn't straighten it out that he would. I told Max that Miami Sizzle was my last rendezvous with you guys. However, he found out that I linked up with you guys a couple more times after Miami. I only went because I was going to get the ring back to show Max that I was serious and sorrowful for what I had done. I couldn't ask you for the ring back. I didn't know how, that's why I just left it alone."

"Where the HELL IS MAX, ROBBIE?! Call the fucking police NOW!"

"Yes, Tony, I'm going to call the police right now." Robbie took his phone out of his purse and called 911. "Max is at his other property, Tony. I told him to meet me there so we could talk. I knew something was wrong when I kept calling you and texting you. Jacob and the guys didn't know what happened to you. It was as if you fell off the planet. When Jerimiah showed me the text that he got about you going to the Caribbeans, I knew something was off. It didn't sound like you but more like something that Max would text. After investigating and questioning Max, he finally confessed. He didn't tell me everything, but he told me enough for me to put the pieces of the puzzle together."

The door suddenly swung open, bouncing off the mattress, and slamming closed as Max hurriedly entered the room. Robbie and I both jumped out of surprise but mostly out of fear.

"YOU DUMB LITTLE SHIT! THIS IS EXACTLY WHY I HAVE A TRACKER ON YOUR FUCKING PHONE AND MY FUCKING CAR! YOU CAN'T BE TRUSTED! SO, THIS IS HOW YOU DO ME, ROBBIE! THIS IS WHAT YOU THINK OF ME?! WHAT THE HELL DO YOU MEAN, *YOU NEVER LOVED ME*? YOU LOVE ANTONIO?! THIS YELLOW ASS FAGGOT IS THE ONE THAT YOU WANT?! YOU WASN'T INTERESTED IN ME AT ALL AFTER ALL THESE FUCKING YEARS?! YOU TOLD ME YOU WERE SORRY! YOU STOOD THERE AND CRIED RIGHT IN FRONT OF MY FACE AND TOLD ME YOU WERE SORRY AND THAT YOU WANTED TO MOVE FORWARD AND LEAVE THE PAST IN THE PAST! I FUCKING BELIEVED YOU, ROBBIE! WE'VE BEEN TOGETHER FOR NINE

FUCKING YEARS AND YOU WANT TO THROW IT ALL AWAY FOR A HOOD RAT?!

Max's rage sent chills through me from my head to my toes. My heart was palpitating as my head and palms sweated profusely! All wishes, hope, faith, and dreams of being rescued escaped me and left me feeling abandoned! I couldn't reach them anymore, my arms were too short to touch any hope anymore. I couldn't think anymore because my mind was too feeble to have any faith, my eyes were too dull to perceive any dreams anymore. Despite it all, I decided that my SPIRIT wasn't faint and decided not to give up. I lay there in total disbelief and anger! *This is not right. This can't be right!* My heart hated God at that very moment, but I shouted out . . .

"GOD, SAVE ME!"

I didn't know what I was asking for or begging for. I just wanted out. I wanted to be rescued once and for all. All of me from the very depths of my soul, I wanted to be unshackled, unbound, and captured. FREED from that bed once and for all. That filthy, dingy, pissy, repulsive bed.

"ANSWER ME GOT DAMMIT!" Max ranted on. "YOU JUST HAD A WHOLE LOT TO SAY A MINUTE AGO! FINISH TELLING HIM HOW MUCH YOU LOVE HIM! TELL HIM MORE ABOUT HOW YOU WANT HIM AND ONLY HIM! I WATCHED AND HEARD EVERY FUCKING THING YOU SAID ON SURVEILLANCE! DO YOU LOVE HIM MORE THAN ME, ROBBIE?!" Max speedily walked over to Robbie and cornered him as Robbie began to cower over in fright before him. "I SAID ANSWER ME GOT DAMMIT! DO YOU WANT TO THROW AWAY NINE FUCKING YEARS FOR THIS MOTHA . . ." *SLAP!* Max slapped Robbie to the floor. ". . .FUCKER! ANSWER ME, ROBBIE, OR I SWEAR I WILL—"

"NOOO, NOOOOOO, MAX!" Robbie screamed out in terror of being slapped again.

Robbie's plea sent chills of fear through me that was so overwhelming, I pissed myself.

Max picked Robbie up off the floor with his hands wrapped around Robbie's neck. Robbie's feet dangled in the air as he struggled to pull Max's hands from his neck. He just hung there in the bare hands of the beast in the corner of the room.

"LET HIM GOOO DAMMIT! LET... LE... LET HIM GO, MOTHERFUCKER!" I yelled, trying to sit up as much as the shackles would allow me.

"SHUT THE FUCK UP, ANTONIO, YOU'RE NEXT!" Max yelled back, looking at me with blood shot eyes of pure exasperation.

I just knew he was going to kill Robbie right in front of me. He continued yelling at Robbie and shaking his lifeless body off of the floor. I cried and begged for him not to kill Robbie. "Please not Robbie, please Lord not Robbie," I prayed.

"Let him go, please let him go. Don't kill him, Max!" I begged and pleaded as tears flowed down my face.

Max turned and looked at me with nothing but evilness and opened his hands, releasing Robbie's spiritless body to fall to the floor. All I heard was a thump and no sound from Robbie. I sat there moving from side-to-side, weeping and trying to see where Robbie was. Hoping and praying that he wasn't dead, but I couldn't help but to believe that he was. I was tired of hoping and praying. I was tired of everything. Nothing seemed to be on my side. All the cards were stacked against me. I was in an uphill battle, and I was constantly sliding down into more and more turmoil.

"I'll be back for your ass next, Antonio!" Max threatened. "I'm going to make sure your demise is much more painful and longer than Robbie's! You'll have him for eternity in HELL! YOU MOTHERFUCKERS DESERVE EACH OTHER!"

Max casually walked out of the room without saying another word. He left, leaving the door fully open. The beast walked out of the room to get Lord knows what. He was gone and there wasn't anything that I could do but lay there in my own piss. I didn't know if I should be a little relieved or more frightened. I didn't know how to feel or what to do! What was he going to do to me when he got back? How long was he going to be gone? Okay, okay, I still didn't hear any sirens. I DIDN'T HEAR ANY SIRENS, THAT'S NOT GOOD! Okay, okay, that just means the police ain't got here yet. They just ain't got here yet that's all! Robbie called them. He called the police and the paramedics. Robbie had to get up now that Max was gone. He can't be dead.

"Robbie . . . Robbie," I whispered as quietly as I could. "Robbie . . . Robbie, get up. Get up. Wake up."

SQEEEAAAK! SQEEEAAAAK!

The cart. IT'S THE CART! I thought to myself. He's coming with that fucking cart again! Past experiences taught me since I been there, that whenever he rolled that cart into the room, there was hell for me to pay.

"ROBBIE . . . ROBBIE . . . ROBBIE!" I raised my voice as I heard the cart roll closer.

Who's shadow is on the wall . . .

CHAPTER XII

The Shadow On The Wall

"ROBBIE . . . ROBBIE!" I continued to yell until I caught myself. At that moment, I had to catch myself because that BEAST could probably hear me. I had to calm down. One of the things I hated was seeing people panic in tough situations. I always felt I could handle anything and there was nothing life could put on my plate that I couldn't handle. I've made it this far. But such fear and torment I never had to deal with. I've never been in a situation like this before. I've never been so scared in my life. I had never . . .

I started to . . . to feel chills suddenly, much colder than usual. I was freezing and sweating at the same time. My heart was pounding hard. My breathing became rapid and deep. As I inhaled and exhaled, my body shivered and my teeth chattered. In an attempt to keep them from rattling, I tried to grind them to keep them together, but the more I tried the more it was useless. I didn't feel good. My stomach was turning. I didn't feel right. Nooooo, noooo, something isn't right. I felt strange. I was having a panic attack, but this time it felt different. It was more intense! I . . . I was expecting the worst. Max is going to kill me. He killed Robbie. HE KILLED ROBBIE! HE'S GOING TO KILL ME AND THEN KILL HIMSELF BEFORE THE POLICE GETS HERE! THE POLICE ARE NOT GOING TO MAKE IT HERE ON TIME!

This is the way that I'm going to die. Dirty, pissy, hungry, and away from my family and loved ones. No one is going to miss me. No one was going to save me. Robbie was the only one that understood me. He was the only one that really loved me and now he's dead. Jerimiah only loved me when it was convenient for him to do so. It's such a shame, Robbie loved me too much, and Jerimiah didn't love me enough. I didn't love Robbie enough and I loved Jerimiah too much. This is the bed that I'm going to die on. How fucking humiliating.

My anticipation for the worst was getting the best of me, and I couldn't stop it. I couldn't do anything about it but lay there and wait for that beast to kill me. It was too much energy for me to try to be optimistic anymore, it was too hard for me. I don't care. I don't give a fuck ANYMORE. Karma was going to repay me for everything I did, for everyone that I hurt. I did dirt, I did wrong but, but MOTHERFUCKA'S have been doing me WRONG ALL MY FUCKING LIFE! My mama, my daddy, my fucking family, and my so-called friends. Robbie's been hiding this shit from me all these years. We were supposed to be homies, lovers, and best friends.

Wait, there is someone . . . a shadow. There's a shadow on the wall. Right where . . .

ROBBIE. It's Robbie. He was . . .

SQUEEEEAK! The squeaking cart in the hall again. It stopped. I paused for a brief second, then . . .

I saw Robbie struggling to stand up. "Get down, Robbie, lay back down. Max is coming. He's coming," I whispered as low as I could.

I believed Robbie saw the fear in my eyes just as much as I could see the fear in his eyes. Before I could warn him anymore, Max entered the room. Robbie quickly laid back down on the floor. How did we get in this mess? Why the hell was I pulled into this bullshit? Robbie, man fucking Robbie.

I can't believe he's been with Max for nine years, and I didn't have a clue about it. How could he put up with such an insecure psychopath for all those years. When I met Robbie five years ago, he was twenty years old. If he's been with Max for nine years, that means he was fifteen or sixteen. Max's Grindr profile says he's thirty-five, which means he was about twenty-five when he got with Robbie. I can't judge Robbie because I did the same shit when I was young. I can sympathize and empathize with him so much on so many things. We've both been taken advantage of by much older men. Our vulnerability and our innocence were taken, but it was also partially given because we allowed it to be taken.

It was our getaway from the flawed, broken, chaotic dwellings that were supposed to be our safe space. No food at home, electricity repeatedly being shut off, no structure or stability was enough to make anyone want to leave. Neither of us had functional homes or upbringings. Homes without fathers or any type of positive male role models. Constant neglect from our fathers and mothers because they were either drunk, high, depressed, or just not home. The rejection that my mom's sperm donor, my father, made me feel when I wanted a relationship with him and he didn't want the same will always be a hurtful feeling. Introduced to sex, violence, alcoholism, drug addicts, abandonment, caused PTSD way too young to comprehend that that shit wasn't right or normal.

I didn't know what PTSD, panic attacks, or anxiety was until Jerimiah explained it to me. He opened my eyes to the abnormality of my upbringing. Jerimiah was wrong on so many levels for picking me up that day, but I wanted to escape from all the bullshit that I was dealing with at that time. At least Jerimiah didn't hurt me or ever tried to control me. He treated me with kindness and respect. Robbie got himself into a hell of a situation and got me caught up in it. I hate him for this. How can I forgive him? How could I ever forgive him for all the shit that Max has done to me? I hate them both. I was too greedy. I should have left Max on read. Robbie should have . . .

SIRENS! The police are coming. They're coming for me. I can hear the sirens approaching. They're coming for me. Everything is going to be okay after all. Everything is fine, it's . . . it's fine. Max can't do anything anymore, it's over. He's busted. I hope he rot in prison for the rest of his fucking miserable life. He doesn't have time to do anything. The police are FINALLY HERE!

CHAPTER XIII

The Cost Of Freedom

Max saw the excitement in my eyes. The emotions and the expression of relief that were written all over my face. My eyes began to swell and instantly water. Max saw my hopes, my wishes, my dreams, and MY PRAYERS being answered. Max stood there and stared at me. He saw my eyes as they secretly attempted to look where Robbie was lying. The sirens were getting louder. It felt as if the vibrations of the sirens were echoing through me. I was afraid not knowing how all of this was going to play out. The noise was so loud it was as if they pulled up right down that hallway. Seconds later, there was knocking at the door. The police were calling for Robbie.

KNOCK! KNOCK! KNOCK!

"Mr. Webster, Robbie Webster!" the police called out.

Max looked at me with panic in his eyes. "Don't say a word! I promise you, Antonio, I will slit your frickin throat ear to ear before they even make it down here," Max threatened me, grabbing the scalpel off the cart.

He pressed the scalpel against my neck, rubbing it up and down. As soon as that cold metal touched my flesh, I knew how sharp it was without feeling it cut me. The coldness of my blood began to drizzle and trickle down to my chest as Max's nervous hand shook.

"Antonio, I will cut around your neck clean to the bone before they can get one step in this room! Do you understand me? I will kill you before they can get to me! DO YOU UNDERSTAND ME, ANTONIO?"

"Ye... ye... yes, Max. I, uh... uh... understand."

BANG! BANG! BANG! The knocks at the door became louder and demanding.

"Robbie Webster and you in there?! We received a 911 call about a domestic disturbance at this address!" the police shouted.

"I'm going to let you live. Yeah, I'm going to let you go, Antonio. Just stay cool. I'm... I'm just going to go to the door just to assure them that everything is fine. Everything is fine, everything is okay. Just relax."

Max walked away from me, placed the scalpel in his coat pocket, and started pacing around the room. The banging upstairs got louder as Max hesitantly made a move towards the basement room door.

"I'm coming, I'm coming!" Max shouted as properly and clearly as he could, trying not to sound highly strung. "I'll be right back, Antonio, and I will unlock you from the shackles. Just relax. I'll be right back."

I could see the concern in Max's face and hear the unrest in his cracking voice as he was talking and walking towards the door looking back at me. His arrogance diminished. He was no longer the cocky motherfucker that he had been since this ordeal started. Max looked at me, gesturing that I be quiet by placing his finger over his mouth as he walked out, gently closing the door behind him.

Not a second after the door closed, I screamed, yelled, hollered, and cried out, "I'M IN HERE! HELP ME, SAVE ME, HEEELLPP, HEEEELLPP!

Before I could shout another plea, Max ran back into the room. Immediately hovering over me reaching into his pockets trying to grab what I'm sure was the scalpel. The knocking and the banging at the door intensified. It sounded as if they were trying to break down the door. I screamed and yelled as loud as I could. I couldn't hear a word that Max was saying anymore. He pressed his hand over my mouth to silence me. I bit it. I crunched down as hard as I could and bit into his hand. Max hollered in pain and tried to snatch his hand away. He scrambled to search for that scalpel in his coat pocket and cut himself, blood immediately seeped through his white coat pocket.

There was nothing he could do with his other hand that was still in my mouth. I bit down harder and harder the more he tussled trying to remove his hand. Max cried out again as he felt my teeth pierce through his skin. When I drew his blood, I clamped into his hand until my teeth felt his bone. Max pleaded like a victim, like the victim that I was, like the victim he made me, until he fucking took . . .

Robbie jumped up. Courage met fear, and fear met courage.

"HE GOT THE KNIFE!" I shouted to Robbie.

Robbie jumped on Max's back and started beating him on the head. I heard the door break open upstairs and what sounded like an army running through the house.

"WE'RE IN THE BASEMENT! HELP! HEEELLP! WE'RE DOWNSTAIRS IN THE BASEMENT!" Robbie yelled as I watched him continue to beat Max.

"WHAT THE FUCK IS GOING ON IN HERE? GET OFF HIM, GET DOWN NOW!" Officer one commanded.

Max snatched his hand from my mouth, leaving part of his flesh lingering and his blood dripping from my lips. Robbie was still on Max's back, beating him with one hand while holding himself up with his arm wrapped around Max's neck. Max struggled to get Robbie off his back as his hands bled all over the place. He continued trying to grab the scalpel out of his pocket. The officers yelled again for Robbie to get off of Max. Robbie didn't hear or wasn't listening. He was in a zone where I don't believe he was able to hear anything at all.

"YOU BASTARD, I HATE YOU! I HATE YOU!" Robbie screamed at Max.

Max aggressively swung around, and Robbie lost his grip and fell against the wall. Just as quickly as Robbie fell, it was just as quick he jumped to his feet and ran back towards Max. Max pulled the scalpel from his pocket and ran towards me.

"STOP, FREEZE! FREEZE GOT DAMMIIT OR I WILL SHOOT YOUR ASS!" Officer one hollered.

I didn't know if they were talking to Max or Robbie. They were both behind me scuffling, and I couldn't turn around enough to see what the hell was going on. Suddenly . . .

POW! POW! POW!

I saw and heard the officers firing their weapons, then I heard a thud on the floor. Max's body flopped over my chest.

"What the fuck just happened?"

"Suspects DOWN!" Officer one called out.

"Where's Robbie? Is he okay?" I asked the officers.

Max began to move. Moving his head from my chest to my stomach made me jump in a way to push his body off me.

"GET HIM OFF ME! GET HIM!" I screamed at the policemen.

It seemed as if the police were moving in slow motion to grab Max off me, and Max seemed to have been moving in fast motion. He moved his head and positioned it underneath my robe and bit down on my penis so hard that I couldn't whimper. I sat up, still limited by the shackles, with my head straight up as my eyes looked at the ceiling and tears streamed down my face. My mouth was wide open, but I couldn't make a sound. It felt as if I was going to pass out. When my head finally dropped, I saw the paramedics working on Robbie and at least three or four officers beating Max. The more the cops tried to pull Max off me, the more I could feel his teeth puncturing into my skin.

"SIR, SIR, IF YOU DON'T RELEASE HIM, I WILL FIRE MY WEAPON! I WILL FUCKING SHOOT YOU, SIR! LET HIM GO GOT DAMMIT!" Officer two demanded.

Max moved, but he did not release my penis from his mouth. Seeing his head move up, Max stretched my penis with his teeth.

"Oooooh, GOD, no, nooo, nooo!" I cried as I saw Max's hand raise up with the scalpel.

POW! POW! POW! POW!

SWOOOOOSSSH!

With one swift swoop of his hand, my princess, my penis was cut completely off and was in Max's mouth. That beast had my severed DICK in his mouth. He stared at me like a deranged mad man smiling with blood all over his face. I watched him as he gagged in attempt to swallow my detached penis. The officers swore and yelled at him to spit it out while beating him. I could no longer feel anything. I thought to myself, *it's finally over and I'm DONE.* There's no coming back from this. My life is over. After all I've been through. After all the shit I've been through, this is what I get. This is what I deserve. I didn't ask to be born. As I laid there in that pissy, bloody, ass bed thinking, I welcomed death.

I welcomed death with opened arms. DEATH, WHERE ARE YOU! I DIDN'T FUCKING ASK FOR THIS SHIT! But I dealt with it. I dealt with it, and I made something out of that shit of a life that I was given. Now, I have to deal with this. I can't. I can't deal with it. I can't take THIS. After all I've been through. As I shook my head in disbelief, my body began to go into shock. I felt so tense and stiff, but I was shaking as if I was having a seizure.

"Relax, sir, relax. Calm down," Paramedic one asked of me. "I want you to concentrate on your breathing. We're going to get you out of here, just hold on! Give me his vitals?"

His voice sounded as if he was miles away from me. Death was near. I called for her, and I was ready for her no matter the cost. I wanted freedom from this fucked up life of mine once and for all.

CHAPTER XIV

Into Shock

"Low blood pressure, shallow breathing, and rapid heartbeat, he's going into shock!" Paramedic two said.

My eyes were glossy, and I felt nauseated. I could see one of the EMT's administering CPR on Max. Robbie was out of my sight. Max stared at me with his deranged eyes still intimidating me. The EMT's vigorously worked on him, trying to save his pathetic life.

"LET HIM CHOKE ON IT AND DIE! LET HIM DIE!" I told them.

"CALM YOURSELF! Sir, you must calm down, OR you are going to die! You're going into shock! You must relax. I'm going to have to administer you with a sedative. It will help."

My eyes lost focus on that beast and they locked in on the needle that the paramedic tapped in preparation to use on me. "NO, NO, NOOO, DON'T, PLEASE DON'T!" I cried. "I don't need it! I don't want any more needles. Please no more!" My head was spinning. My thoughts were bouncing all over the place. I was swimming in confusion. "NOOOO, DON'T, PLEASE . . . please, please." My shouting suddenly lowered.

I couldn't fight them off, I was too weak. I knew he stuck me with that fucking needle because I once again felt the warmth of the serum flowing into my blood stream. It brought my mind and body somewhat peace. With my eyes still open, I watched him hand the needle to the other paramedic. They didn't give a damn about me. They were just doing their job. How could anyone know how much I was tortured by Max, let alone how much I wanted to watch him be unalived! Looking at him, I could see he wanted just as much to watch me be unalived. Sooo much hatred, so much anger, hurt, and pain. Laying there frozen, I couldn't help but to place myself in Max shoes.

What would I have done if I found out that the person I was in love with, engaged to, did me like Robbie did him. The type of person that I am and has always been, I would have taken it to the next level of pettiness. I would have fucked his closet family members. I would have done him dirty and hurt him by any means necessary. Max was so mean and cruel to Robbie, so I see why he did what he did. I didn't even know Robbie was in a relationship, let alone engaged! Knowing myself, sadly, it wouldn't have made a difference if I knew or didn't. I was selfish and greedy. Whatever I wanted, whoever I wanted, I eventually got.

My thoughts began to consume me into a different realm. Max's coughing snapped me out of it.

"I got it," Paramedic three said. "Hand me the bag."

I watched the paramedic with his purple gloves place my penis in a clear bag, then into an ice chest.

I dropped my head while the paramedics worked on cleaning me up. While moving me onto a stretcher, I was finally able to see Robbie. I watched silently mourning as tears rolled down my face as they covered his body with a white sheet. I reached out to touch him as they carried him out of the room. Two policemen walked behind his body while escorting Max out, handcuffed to a gurney.

"It's his fault! All of this is his fault!" Max screamed, pointing at me. "It's his frickin fault! Robbie and I had a great relationship before he came along and ruined it! We were happy and fine. We both sacrificed our selfishness to become a unit! I gave up everything to build a great life for us! Whatever he needed, I made sure he had it. Whatever he wanted. He didn't want for anything because I made sure he had it without him asking! I took this house from my parents and placed them in a nursing home because Robbie wanted to live here. He wanted to be back down south to be close to his family! I didn't even see my family at all.

I moved back down here in this dirty ass red-neck state for Robbie! It was for him. It was all for him! I came out of the closet to my family and friends because he wanted me to! I did this, all of this for us, so we could have a place to call home! So that he could have stability in his life. Some comfort and peace for him. Some serenity inside and away from the chaos outside. We were perfect until HE came into the picture! How could something so perfect end this way! It can't end. I won't let it end! WE ARE SOULMATES! I loved him, I love him! Robbie, I love you, I love you, babe! Robbie, Robbie! Please, forgive me! Don't go! I need you! Robbie! I forgive you! I forgive you! Please forgive me!" Max pleaded as his voice faded away from the hearing range of my ears.

When I walked outside, all of my pain was gone. The brightness was blinding. It was hard to keep my eyes open at first, but they adjusted. Peace and harmony were all around me. No longer did I feel angry, hate, or abandoned. I felt unconditional love, and I was grateful for everything, even though I didn't understand everything; now I do. Now, I understand.

www.ingramcontent.com/pod-product-compliance
Lightning Source LLC
Chambersburg PA
CBHW040828010826
48978CB00012BB/648